ACCENT ON MURDER

BOOK 3 OF THE STRANDED IN PROVENCE
MYSTERIES

SUSAN KIERNAN-LEWIS

D1366261

SAN MARCO PRESS

Books by Susan Kiernan-Lewis

The Maggie Newberry Mysteries
Murder in the South of France
Murder à la Carte
Murder in Provence
Murder in Paris
Murder in Aix
Murder in Nice
Murder in the Latin Quarter
Murder in the Abbey
Murder in the Bistro
Murder in Cannes
Murder in Grenoble
Murder in the Vineyard
Murder in Arles
Murder in Marseille
Murder in St-Rémy
Murder à la Mode
Murder in Avignon
Murder in the Lavender
A Provençal Christmas: A Short Story
A Thanksgiving in Provence
Laurent's Kitchen

An American in Paris Mysteries
Déjà Dead
Death by Cliché
Dying to be French
Ménage à Murder

The Stranded in Provence Mysteries
Parlez-Vous Murder?
Crime and Croissants
Accent on Murder
A Bad Éclair Day
Croak, Monsieur!
Death du Jour
Murder Très Gauche
Wined and Died
A French Country Christmas

The Irish End Games
Free Falling
Going Gone
Heading Home
Blind Sided
Rising Tides
Cold Comfort
Never Never
Wit's End
Dead On
White Out
Black Out
End Game

The Mia Kazmaroff Mysteries
Reckless
Shameless
Breathless
Heartless
Clueless
Ruthless

Ella Out of Time
Swept Away
Carried Away
Stolen Away

The French Women's Diet

1

ONCE BURNED

Pauline Toule held the wind-up toy in the palm of her hand.

It was the figure of a little Frenchman complete with beret and a baton of bread that he held in his fist. Before the toy was broken, when one wound it up the little man would wave the baton in agitation. Pauline often wondered what rationale the toymaker had employed that would prompt him to create an angry toy for the amusement of children.

Did the toymaker imagine it would give children an illusion of power over the irate adults in their lives?

Pauline placed the toy on the nightstand by her bed. Years ago, when she'd taught only girls, this toy had been passed around and played with by the students for many years. The first day of the first semester of teaching boys, it broke.

Why had she kept it all these years?

She turned the light out and lay her head down on her pillow, praying sleep would come tonight. She could hear the sounds of the children playing outside her window, faint but there. Her house used to be on the outskirts of Chabanel. Now it was nearly at its center.

She turned in her bed to see if another position might be more conducive to sleep. She was heavy and repositioning left her sweating and enervated.

She listened to the sounds of her breathing, labored and wheezing from the effort of turning in her bed.

She knew very well why she'd kept the broken toy.

It was to remind her of how horrible boys were.

How horrible they all were.

Thank God I was able to prove that the Italian bottle washer at the Bar á GoGo was tippling the sherry. Because if I hadn't, I'd be drinking dandelion wine by now or, worse —*les soeurs'* nearly undrinkable blackberry wine.

I held up my glass of *kir* in a toast to Katrine who sat across from me. She lifted her own glass of rosé wine.

But since I *had* in fact uncovered the sherry thief, I'd been paid for my efforts by the owner of the bar, Romain Armand, to the tune of two free glasses of *kir* a day for six months.

Viva la apocalypse.

"What are we toasting?" Katrine asked blowing out a stream of cigarette smoke into the already smoky room.

Katrine Pelletier was my closest friend in Chabanel —the French village where I'd gone on vacation and then gotten stranded in when an EMP went off over the Mediterranean. She and her husband Gaultier make and sell cheese and trust me there are a lot worse friends to have during a worldwide economic downturn.

"How about being alive?" I said, sipping my drink, trying to make it last. It was already my second one.

"Over rated," Katrine said, knocking back most of her wine. "I need more."

I was pretty sure she didn't mean wine, although in truth, probably that too. The fact was there was something up with Katrine—honestly there had been since the first day we met when she confessed to me that the only reason she'd befriended me was because I looked like her husband's ex-wife and she wanted to get in front of anything that might happen between me and Gaultier.

As if. The guy was nice and all but he had a distinct resemblance to one of the goats he and Katrine raised.

But I'm being nice at the moment. After all, I'm two glasses of *kir* into my day.

It was a pleasantly cool day in early September and while normally I'd have opted to sit outside, it was also threatening rain and my faux-Prada flats do not do well in puddles. Even south of France puddles.

As it was I was spending a good deal of brain power trying to imagine how I was going to peddle all the way back to *La Fleurette* without taking the foolish things off and stuffing them inside my denim jacket.

La Fleurette is this giant ancient *mas* I live in on the outskirts of the village. I live there with two old ladies—neither of whom speak English—two cats and a dog. I'm sure there are other assorted varmints I'm not counting but I don't like to think of that.

I have never been an outdoor girl in any sense of the word and if you'd told me six months ago that I would willingly move to a farm in the French countryside, I'd be forced to remind you to take whatever Alzheimer's medicine you clearly forgot to take.

And yet. *Voila*, as they say around here. I live on a farm with two ninety-plus year old twins. Without electricity, running water or cable.

But back to Katrine's problem.

"I need a life," Katrine said, frowning into her drink. "Without kids. Without a husband. And while we're wishing, some place different."

"But except for those things, everything is okay?"

She raised an eyebrow at me. "I love my kids," she said dutifully.

"And your husband."

"Yes, yes," she said with a sigh. "Him, too."

"You probably just need a vacation from selling cheese all day. Honestly, I've been meaning to mention to you that you're starting to smell like Gorgonzola."

"Why did I ever learn English to be subjected to your wit?"

"Fear not," I said, wistfully polishing off the last of my *kir*, "I'm taking French lessons now."

"You're kidding."

"I wish I was. The Madame Twins are making me do it."

"How long?"

"I've been enduring it...er, doing it...exactly two days now."

"And your French is still terrible. Who's teaching you?"

"Madame Toule. Do you know her?"

"Everybody knows her. She was the school mistress in Chabanel for two decades."

"I hope her attitude was a little better when she was teaching children," I said. "She's pretty dour."

"I don't know that word. Does it mean fat?"

I laughed. Madame Toule was indeed overweight, in fact morbidly obese—something you don't see much of in

France, regardless of the fact that the food pretty much makes you want to eat all the time.

"No. She's unhappy," I said.

"Oh. Dour. Unhappy. Okay."

"Loose translation."

Katrine leaned forward, her eyes sparkling for the first time since she'd sat down.

"She has reason to be dour," she said, practically rubbing her hands together in anticipation of the gossip she clearly had to tell.

"I'm all ears."

"Years ago she slept with a student."

I frowned. "How old a student?"

"Thirteen? Maybe twelve," Katrine said with a shrug.

"Did she lose her job?"

"What for? Besides, it was never proven."

"So it's just gossip?"

"Do you have a saying in America about there usually being fire if you smell smoke?"

"Yeah, okay, so everybody believed she did it but she never paid the price."

"Oh, she paid a price all right. I had her the year after this all happened and I never saw an unhappier person. My husband Gaultier had her the year before and he said she was always laughing and telling funny stories. So something *definitely* happened."

"Wow. Poor dear. Was she always so...big?"

"*Mais oui*. Always fat but no longer jolly," Katrine said sadly.

"Which just goes to show that things don't always follow the stereotype," I said staring at my empty glass.

"How about you?" Katrine said signaling to the waiter to bring two more drinks. "You and Luc not going forward?"

I was torn between frustration at having to answer that question when Luc and I so clearly *should* have been going forward and anticipation at the fact that I did in fact have time for one more *kir*.

"I just don't get it," I said. "He comes to *La Fleurette* a lot. He's coming tonight in fact. And we get along great."

"But?"

"But nothing. It's like we're stalled or something."

"Perhaps you should jump him."

"Right. Because that's what a French girl would do, right?"

"Why do you care what a French girl would do? He clearly likes you because you're an American girl."

2

THE LESS WE KNOW

C hief Luc DeBray walked across his office and poked his head in the hallway. His sergeant Eloise Basile was sitting in the foyer between an elderly farmer and his wife. Luc wasn't sure what kind of problem they were trying to work out but whatever it was he had faith that Eloise's light touch was the right approach.

It had been four months since the EMP and once everyone realized they'd probably survive going forward and only had to give up their cable TVs and the Internet—things bizarrely had gotten more tense. Luc would leave the reasons for that to the psychologists.

He had a village to keep safe. He'd learned a long time ago that if he didn't worry about *why* people behaved the way they did, but only dealt with their behavior, he would save himself a lot of trouble.

"Sergeant," he said to Eloise.

She jerked her head up in alert attention.

"Yes, Chief?"

"Go home at the regular time tonight. Matteo is on duty."

"Yes, Chief."

Luc turned back to his office. Out his window the plane tree was losing its leaves. Autumn would soon come to Provence.

How would that change things in the village?

It was only around five in the afternoon but already Luc found himself thinking of *La Fleurette* and his planned visit there this evening.

He wasn't sure what he was doing with Jules. He had a gut feeling that he should stay away—treat her like any other villager. He knew there could be no future with her. Some day she would leave and go back to her own country.

He felt a tremor of excitement at the thought of Jules indefinitely trapped in France and scolded himself for even thinking it.

Would he want her to stay because she couldn't leave? Wouldn't she always yearn to go home?

No. Even if she stayed, she'd be unhappy. And if she left, well...it was clearly best for all concerned not to put too many beignets in *that* basket.

His phone rang—a rarity now in France, indeed in all of Europe—and he picked up the receiver with trepidation.

"Chief DeBray."

"Luc, it's Jean-Paul." Jean-Paul Tourner had been Luc's liason in Aix but had recently transferred to Nice. Although technically Luc's superior the two got along well.

"We have a problem," Jean-Paul said.

Luc tensed. Those words would have meant something totally different four months ago before the EMP changed all their lives. Since then Luc had revised his definition of what a problem was.

"What's happened?"

"It's the ring road black market around Nice. We've got three more murders there."

Luc knew the Nice black market was bad news. The lowest level of the French criminal element had adopted the market and turned it into something very dangerous. Because the prices at the market were so high, the situation, unsurprisingly, also worked for the average Niçoise citizen hoping to trade or buy goods.

Unfortunately, the body count for the market was rising every day.

"Any leads?" Luc asked, running a hand through his hair. The last thing he needed was for something like this to get anywhere near Chabanel. He hated to think it but a part of him was relieved it was contained to Nice and its environs.

"None. The bastards pack up as if they'd never been there and relocate the next week to a different section of the ring road."

"How are they getting the word out to people who come to trade?"

"Word of mouth. I'm working on getting someone on the inside but it's taking time."

And in the meantime, people are dying.

"What can I do for you?"

"Tell your people to stay away. Making a fast buck won't help them if they're dead. Get the word out."

"Will do, Jean-Paul," Luc said feeling a rush of gratitude that at least this was one thing he didn't have on his plate to worry about.

~

I tried to put my finger on exactly why these French lessons were so onerous.

It could be the omnipresent stench of mothballs and lavender cakes that seemed to float in the air in Madame Toule's house like a visible stratum of pollution. It could be the ponderous, cumbrous way that Madame Toule moved—whether it was her body or even just her hands—as if she were weighed down by andirons.

Or it could be because Madame Toule refused to speak a word of English during our lessons—even though I know she spoke it well.

I told her I could hardly learn by immersion if I was only immersed one hour a day but she was very stubborn about not speaking English to me.

As a result I ended up holding my nose and feeling generally lost from the moment I walked into Madame Toule's little house until the moment I gained sweet, release into the cobblestone lane out her front door.

It was a charming little house even if it looked as if it had been staged in the 1950s. I don't know if Madame Toule was a spinster or just divorced a long time ago but the place had a definite feel of no-man-around-the-place. Not to be sexist but that generally meant things were falling down.

There was a strip of missing wallpaper in the living room that ran half way down the wall, a hole above where the phone was affixed to the wall—like you'd see in museums circa 1925—and a broken leg on the couch that had an old dictionary shoved under it to keep it balanced.

I like to think I can tell things about people just by watching them—even if they don't speak my language. But I've learned the hard way that insane or depressed people are impossible to read. Their eyes give nothing away. Their movements reveal no intent or purpose because they basically have none. When you add to all that the fact that the subject is five foot two and weighs two hundred and fifty pounds you have a recipe for a classic enigma.

Greta Garbo, not so much, but Madame Toule was still a mystery. A tragic figure. A woman surrounded in secrets. A lover of young boys and high-calorie food.

And that's another thing. With somebody this big you'd expect to see chips packets or homemade brownies or empty pizza boxes everywhere. But I got the idea that she rarely went out and I never detected a hint of baked goods or any other kind of cooking in her house.

Maybe she's not really fat? Maybe it's an undiagnosed tumor?

"*Attention, s'il vous plait, Madame Hooker.*"

"Call me Jules."

"*Répétez,*" she said, ignoring my request as she always did. "*La chèvre a sauté sur la clôture.*"

"La chiffon assaulted Sir lab coat."

"*Non, Madame Hooker. Écoutez, s'il vous plait.*"

This was really agonizing and at the rate we were going I'm positive I'll never learn to speak French. Unfortunately, stopping the lessons was out of the question. The Madame Twins came by every now and then with a basket of tomatoes from the farm or homemade tapenade to see Madame Toule, so it wouldn't take long for them to discover I was ditching class.

Kill me now.

I dutifully attempted to repeat the gobble-de-gook she spoke to me. To be fair, she never gets exasperated when yet again I do not get it right.

We literally go on like this five more times until I'm sure I'm about to scream if she won't stop and put us both out of our misery.

In fact, so aggravated am I that when the noise at the window erupted—inches from my head—a part of me thought it was my head exploding in frustration.

Madame Toule didn't even scream. She just stared dully at the big hole in the window where the rock had come through and which now lay on the worn wool rug at our feet.

I jumped up and ran to the window but the street was empty. Whoever had thrown the rock had plenty of time to dart down any number of nearby alleyways. I turned back to the living room and picked up the rock. It was really just a chunk of cobblestone which made me think the deed might have been more spontaneous than planned.

"Has this happened before?" I asked.

Madame Toule was looking through the window as if she expected to see someone materialize there.

There was no fear or alarm in her eyes. Just sadness.

"Children can be cruel," she said.

3

ABOUT FACE

After I helped Madame Toule clean up the broken glass and position a piece of cardboard in the window, she seemed ready to let the lesson go for the day. I hated feeling grateful to the little weasel who'd thrown the rock through her window but I was glad to have the lesson cut short.

La Fleurette—the *mas* that Luc mysteriously came into some kind of ownership of and then gave to me and *les soeurs* (as he calls the elderly twins)—was a good three miles outside Chabanel. Ask any French person and they'll tell you that's it's a comfortable leg stretch the equivalent of a block or two.

For the rest of the world—*i.e. normal people*—it's a day-long hike requiring provisions and camel bags of water and personally not one I'd willingly agree to do unless I had Japanese soldiers walking beside me jabbing me with bayonets every step of the way.

Which is why I bike it.

Thankfully the rain never materialized so after my drinks with Katrine and my lesson with Madame Toule I didn't have to pedal home barefooted with my favorite shoes stuffed in my jacket pockets.

Thinking of Katrine made me wonder what her evening would be like tonight. I know she's nuts about her husband —when she's not thinking that maybe he could help a little more with the kids—but I also know she's unhappy too. Maybe she thinks *this* is as happy as she deserves to be. Maybe that goes along with being a cheese seller in post-apocalyptic France.

But I think Katrine is unhappy because she knows there's more to life. And she wants it.

The hell of it is, from the outside looking in, Katrine had the main things there was to have in life. She had the loving husband, the cute kids, and she had engaging, fulfilling work. Personally, I wasn't sure there was much more to hope for.

Speaking of those things to hope for, I reminded myself that Luc was coming to dinner tonight. He did that a lot so it wasn't like we'd put out the linen tablecloth and the best silver—as if we had any of those things—but it was still exciting to anticipate.

As close as I like to think Luc and I have come, there are some things we cannot say to each other. There's a hesitancy between us that I think is exclusive to France. If we were in Atlanta, I'd come right out and ask him what's going on between us? And if he were American he would either then *not* totally freak out or he would proceed to back-pedal like mad to escape me. But at least I'd know.

There appeared to be more of a games-playing mentality in French romantic involvements. There were many unspoken rules and to someone who didn't understand the *spoken* rules, that was particularly frustrating.

The *mas* came into view from around the last curve in

the road after I'd left the heart of Chabanel behind me. From this distance it looked like an abandoned hulk on the horizon but the closer you got to it the more it began to resemble a rather pleasing assembly of stones and cement blocks.

It has a long winding unpaved driveway with two deeply rutted tire tracks as if to show the pathway of centuries of horse-drawn wagons.

In front of the house there is a circular drive of pea gravel. The Madame Twins had already crammed every window top and bottom—five of them in all—with boxes of blood red geraniums. There were gargantuan hedges of purple and blue hydrangea flanking the large double wooden door.

It looked pretty grand until you got up close.

Not that I'm complaining. Not a bit. I've been homeless and I've lived in a dump and trust me, the dump is better.

Not that this is a dump. It is a falling down stone farm-house built in the seventeen hundreds. It has mature plant-ings and thick beds of flower and vegetables and fruit trees forming a back garden that Luc and the sisters seem to think will eventually be enough to feed the whole village should that time ever come but certainly enough to feed just us.

All thanks to Luc, our benefactor.

I tossed the bike down on the small strip of crabgrass between the drive and the side path that snaked around the house to the back garden. Luc would walk from Chabanel but instinct still had me parking my bike in places where it wouldn't be likely to get run over.

The minute I entered the back garden, my dog Cocoa launched herself at me. Having never had a dog before growing up I swear I will never get used to the enthusiastic greeting she gives me—and I'm not sure I can ever live without it now that I've had it. I knelt briefly to snuggle her and receive her excited tongue lashing before straightening up.

Léa Cazaly stood in the doorway, a dishtowel in her hands. While the sisters are identical twins most people have no trouble telling them apart because Madame Cazaly always looks bereaved. Recently I've noticed that she's acted much less sad but it's like her face was frozen for so many years in misery that it can't relearn new lines of humor. So it's always easy to spot her. That and the fact that she wears black. Like she's in mourning.

Madame C grimaced at me and rattled off a bunch of French. I walked to her and kissed her on both cheeks.

"I have no idea what you said but I hope whatever it is it rhymes with *dinner's ready*."

She snorted—her way of showing loving amusement with me—and followed me inside toward the tantalizing fragrance of sautéing onions and peppers.

I love evenings the very best in the south of France. I love the way the gold light of the dying sun mixes with the red that's hovering along the horizon.

Maybe that's the wine talking because come to think of it I always seem to have a glass of wine in my hand at this time of day.

The Madame Twins wanted us to eat outside tonight, even though I thought it was getting a little on the chilly side. Supposedly when fall and winter comes to Provence all you can do is remember longingly of the warm summer evenings and the sisters were loathe to begin the process of dining indoors just yet.

I bundled up in my favorite Ralph Lauren sweater and made sure I was sitting close to the grill.

In the States any guy in the equation would automatically man the grill but in France that role is pretty much gender neutral. The old ladies got the dishes of phyllo-wrapped Brie with fig preserves and toasted walnuts ready and I got the fire going using charcoal and sticks.

Little by little it seemed we were getting more things back from that day four months ago when the EMP happened. Already Aix had streetlights up and down the Cours Mirabeau for four hours each evening. They were run by a generator but obviously the city fathers figured there was enough fuel to allow pedestrians to stroll the famous boulevard at night.

Only the French would think that night strolling was a big deal.

I have to admit it's very nice though.

While the Aix hospital always had electricity because of its dedicated generator, the rest of us have been lighting candles and hoarding batteries for our flashlights but the big worry that we'd run out of both had yet to happen.

It seems there's always a candle, a lantern or a battery-operated lamp anywhere you go in Chabanel—from the bars at night to the restaurants to people's homes. And frankly, it's kind of pleasant and cozy.

Luc came onto the terrace from the outside gate. I felt my usual surge of excitement to see him that I tamped down to appear cool and unimpressed. He kissed me on both cheeks and poured himself a glass of wine.

Luc is seriously handsome. He's tall, with brown hair and dark green eyes with thick lashes. Very sexy but doesn't seem to know it.

While we waited for the grill to get hot, the old ladies

finally sat down—something they never do—and joined me and Luc with a glass of sauterne.

I love these two dearly but it's always a godsend when someone is around to translate for us. They must think so too because while normally fairly taciturn, they turn into veritable chatterbugs when someone can actually understand what they're saying.

I poked at the charcoal while Madame Cazaly talked animated to Luc. He was frowning at what I was doing and trying to listen to Madame C.

"You shouldn't move it around too much," he said to me. "Give the wood a chance to burn."

"Did Madame C tell you I'm taking language lessons?" I said, ignoring his comment.

"She said you are not committed to it."

"Madame Toule must be tattling on me," I said, leaning back in my chair and taking possession of my wine glass again. "She thinks I should be further along by now. She refuses to speak English to me."

"That is the whole point, no?" Luc said with a wry smile.

I turned to Madame Becque who had jumped up to season the lamb chops because God forbid she should sit still for longer than five seconds when there was something irrelevant and unnecessary to do.

"Ask one of them about Madame Toule's big secret, would you?" I asked Luc. "Katrine said Madame Toule was scandal fodder not too long ago."

Luc sighed and spoke to *les soeurs*. He seemed to have really lit a match under them because they both began talking at once. I heard the words *Madame Toule* and *tant pis* which I know meant *too bad* with much clucking and head shaking.

Eventually, Luc turned to me and said with a shrug—

and honestly ninety percent of what the man says to me is accompanied with a shrug—"They say Madame Toule has had a hard life."

"That's all you got from that five-minute fusillade?" I said in astonishment. "They must have said more than that. Go back to the well, Chief. Don't go all male on me. I want the good stuff!"

He laughed. "It is just gossip, Jules."

"Exactly! Let's have it!"

Madame Cazaly wagged a finger at me so I guess she got the gist of what I was ragging Luc about. I might as well give up. *Nobody* had more secrets than Madame Cazaly and if the Nazis couldn't get her to talk back in 1943 I was pretty sure I couldn't.

"Can you at least tell me if it's true that Madame Toule was caught sleeping with her twelve-year-old student?"

"I will if you can tell me what possible good it would do for you to know that?"

"You're impossible," I said in exasperation as Madame B spritzed water on the grill and proclaimed it ready—but not before I saw her exchange a covert look with Madame C so I knew for sure there was more on the subject of Madame Toule's secrets than they were telling.

An hour later, the light was gone, the lanterns were lit and the old ladies were happily bustling about our huge eleventh century farmhouse kitchen cleaning up after the dinner.

Luc and I offered to help but they like the ritual of washing and tidying up after a good meal, and Luc and I like the ritual of sitting on the patio with our wine and watching the day wash completely from the sky.

I have to say I would have expected Luc to have made a move before now. Not long ago he'd started calling me *chérie* but then stopped for some reason. I could tell our evenings were not completely in the friend zone. There were too many knowing looks, raised eyebrows and other visual cues that told me that.

I'm not totally insensate. I *can* pick up on basic romantic foreplay.

And yet still nothing was happening. No leaning over to kiss me, no taking my hand to companionably share the evening's alpenglow with me. No murmuring *ma chérie* in my ear.

Nada.

Again, I was trying to figure out how much of his sangfroid was our different cultures and how much was just him.

"*Les soeurs* seem happy," he said as we heard Madame C's laughter drift out to us from the house.

"I think they are," I said. "They like to be busy and boy are they ever now. Plus everybody wants to buy their knitting and their cucumbers and the little chicken pot pies they make."

"I heard about their blackberry wine."

"That means our little social media campaign is working."

He raised an eyebrow at me.

"We've been giving out free samples at the village market," I explained.

"Ahhh. And have you tasted the product yourself?"

"I have. It's delicious *and* it cures warts."

"A wonder drink."

"*Exactement.*"

I was seconds away from saying in my brusquely impatient American way *were we ever going to get this party started?*—crude I know but the French expect no less from us Yanks especially after Trump—when Cocoa began barking and running to the edge of the patio.

The last thing I worried about was an intruder when I had the chief of the Chabanel police department in my house so I was relaxed when my friend Thibault Theroux made his way through the garden gate and onto the patio.

"*Bonsoir*, Chief," he said to Luc and then leaned over to kiss me on both cheeks. "*Bonsoir*, Jules."

"*Bonsoir* to you too, Thibault," I said. "Are you hungry? *Les soeurs* made rosemary and garlic lamb."

If you didn't know Thibault, you would definitely be tempted to cross the street to avoid him. He was unkempt with long stringy hair and one droopy eye, and his clothes always looked liked he'd slept in them.

"*Mais oui*," Thibault said pulling up a chair. He was a big man and even with normal sized furniture he looked like a giant trying to sit in children's chairs. I got up to go inside to make him a plate before the sisters put everything away.

I assembled a large platter of roasted eggplant and tomatoes, drizzled with olive oil and feta cheese, and several warm lamb chops. Madame C poured me a large glass of rosé to bring to him, all of which I carefully balanced in my arms as I made my way back to the dimly lit terrace.

The fact that I was trying not to drop anything, break my neck or run into a door was the only excuse I can give for why I didn't immediately realize the atmosphere on the terrace had drastically changed in the time it took me to leave, fix a plate and return.

I set Thibault's plate and wine glass in front of him but he didn't immediately reach for his fork.

"Is everything okay?" I said, finally twigging that something was up. I glanced at Luc to see if it could be the result of something he had said while I was in the house.

"Our friend Thibault has a surprise for you," Luc said, his face stony.

Whatever kind of surprise it was clearly it didn't involve balloons and ponies or anything nice. I looked at Thibault with building apprehension.

"What is it?" I asked, hugging myself as if to protect against his words.

Thibault had a ham radio and was my only source of information as to what was happening back in the States. Recently he'd said things had improved but now I found myself holding my breath in fear.

"It is a *good* surprise," Thibault said, glancing at Luc as if Luc might argue with him.

Luc was staring at his wine glass and I was bewildered at his change of manner.

What in the world could have happened?

"There is a boat leaving Marseille tomorrow night," Thibault said, not looking at me. "It is headed to Miami and they have room for one more."

4

TAKING IT TO THE LIMIT

A t first I didn't understand what Thibault was saying. He acted so dispirited that it wasn't until I reran the tapes of what he'd just said that it hit me.

I could go home!

I grabbed his arms in an effort to twist him around to face me which was a lot like trying to maneuver a small building.

"Who? How?" I sputtered. "Really?"

In the last week, Thibault had told me that the US appeared to be pulling itself together faster than anyone expected. Already they had electricity again. They had communications up and running in all the major cities and they were fashioning a mode of mass transportation that was putting the horse and buggy back in the barns.

It's possible the damage wasn't as bad as previously thought. The fact was while it might still be a little rough around the edges, whatever was happening back home, it was no longer the wild, wild west of just two months ago.

"So you want to go, Jules?" Thibault said.

"Yes! Of course I do," I said, nearly jumping up and down in my excitement.

I was going home! I'd be able to see my mother and CeCe! I could get that job at the paper! My condo! My gorgeous condo with all my clothes! Oh! My Prada shoes! My vintage Louis Vuitton satchel!

I was in such a swirl of imaginings of what my new life would be like back home that I didn't even see Luc and Thibault any more.

"Is it safe?" Luc said quietly.

"The States?" I said, turning to him, my eyes bright with excitement. "Thibault said they've got law and order again. Didn't you Thibault?"

"I meant the boat," Luc said.

"What boat?" I said.

"The boat you would be taking from Marseille to Miami," Luc said. "A sea journey of what? Eight days?" He looked at Thibault who nodded.

"Well, of course it's safe," I said. "I'm sure it's safe. The real question is can I pay for it?" I looked at Thibault.

"They will collect your passage on the other end. You can access your bank account as soon as you land."

"I have money again!" I said, clapping my hands.

The Madame Twins stepped out onto the terrace to see what all the excitement was about which dashed the first bit of cold water on my euphoria.

I would have to tell them I was leaving.

I forced myself not to glance around at this lovely farm or to think of the very comfortable arrangement I had here with them. Surely they would understand.

Thibault was quietly answering their questions in French and I watched their faces go from curiosity to horror.

They looked at me and Madame Cazaly said something to me.

"What did she say?" I asked.

Luc sighed. "She wants to know if you would really leave."

I felt a wave of frustration. *How could she ask that?*

"America is my home," I said to her.

Luc translated and she spoke to him with clear bitterness.

"Tell me what she said."

"She said she thought *this* was your home."

I dug my nails into the palms of my hands and fought down the irrational guilt I felt at being joyful at finally being able to go home.

"No," I said evenly, hoping Luc could soften my words because I didn't have the stomach to. "This is a very nice place to wait until I can get back home."

Remember how I said I loved the evenings best in the south of France? Well, that's because I forgot how gorgeous it is here in the morning. Especially if you've got an espresso in front of you and a fresh chocolate croissant.

I don't think anything else can compare to the start of any day. Plus there's that whole clear blue sky and warm breeze thing going on too.

What *wasn't* so wonderful was the decidedly cold shoulder that Madame Cazaly had decided to bestow upon me.

I was all set to be understanding about her disappointment before she decided to try to make me miserable and refuse to understand how I might want to go back where I came from.

So the next morning after Thibault's visit, I sat alone on the terrace and drank my coffee and ate my sweet roll and felt the sun on my face while enduring the indicting stare of my dog. Well, actually it wasn't so much indicting as a mixture of rancor and begging. Very tricky for most people to pull off but Cocoa was clearly managing it. I fed her at least a third of my roll but I could tell she was still miffed at me.

I was doing my best to avoid Madame C and she, of course, was doing her best to make sure we had as much contact as possible because otherwise how would I know how pissed off she was?

I knew this morning was market day for them and their blackberry wine. In fact I was awakened by the sound of the donkey-pulled milk cart that they'd hired to bring their wine into Chabanel.

I figured I didn't need to actually say final goodbyes until midmorning so my plan was to act all nonchalant, pack my stuff up once the Madame Twins had left for the market and then when Thibault's pal Diego came to pick me up for the drive to Marseille, I'd ask him to swing by the market where I could say my final goodbyes to Katrine and the Madame Twins. And hope that the public venue would prevent Madame C from throwing ripe produce at me as I left.

Saying goodbye to Luc was going to be a whole other proposition and I still hadn't sorted out how I'd manage that. I hadn't wanted to say goodbye to him last night—and I could tell he was in no mood to be sentimental.

I have to tell you I was mildly astounded that all of these so-called friends—with the exception of Thibault—would want to deny me my chance to go back to my own country.

I know France is awesome but come on! Can no one see why I might want to go home? Even to a place that doesn't have amazing croissants and nonstop access to *vin de terroir*?

I fed the last of my croissant to Cocoa and tousled her ears. I hated to leave her but she would be a good guard dog for *les soeurs*.

Still. This dog had literally saved my life.

I stared into her eyes and for a moment I wasn't at all sure I could go through with it.

"Jules, *chérie*?"

I looked up to see Madame Becque standing at the gate. Madame Becque was always the sane one of the two sisters and that was never more true than this morning. I have no idea what she said to me but I bolted out of my chair and ran to her to throw my arms around her.

"I don't want to leave you, Justine," I said, tears streaming down my face. I figured surely now when I was leaving I might be allowed the intimacy of calling her by her first name. "Please try to understand."

"*Je comprends*," Madame B said, patting my shoulder. "*Je comprends*."

"I'll see you again some day," I said. "When the world gets back on its feet. I promise."

She shook her head and her eyes glittered with unshed tears. "*Nous t'aimons*," she said.

We love you.

I tried not to just out and out bawl.

"I love you too," I said, swallowing hard. "*Je vous aime, aussi*."

"Is very good, Jules," she said with a sad smile about my pronunciation. And again, between her and Cocoa, I wasn't at all sure I could go through with this.

The moment was broken by a scream coming from Madame C at the front of the house.

A look of panic jolted across Madame B's face and both of us turned and ran to the front drive. I reached it first. The owner of the donkey cart, Monsieur Augustin, a grizzled old fellow blind in one eye, was standing next to Madame C. He had his hand on her elbow as if afraid she'd topple over any moment and looked at us with immense relief as Madame B and I ran up.

Madame B rattled off questions in French and between Monsieur Augustin and Madame C, the answers she got back made her blanche.

And then look at me.

"What is it?" I asked. "What the hell happened?"

Monsieur Augustin licked his lips as if looking for the right words.

"Why did Madame C scream?"

At the sound of her name Madame C crossed her arms and glowered at me as if I were the one responsible. But her face looked more ashen than angry.

Madame B put her hand on Madame C's shoulder to comfort her.

"Will somebody please tell me what the hell happened?" I said in frustration.

"Is Madame Toule," Monsieur Augustin said, obviously seeing I was about to blow a gasket.

"Madame Toule? Is she hurt?"

He nodded. "I am saying yes. Very much so." He lowered his voice and stepped away from the two sisters who now turned to each other.

He spoke to me in a low voice.

"She is being murdered," he said solemnly.

5

THE SHORT STRAW

The report had come in a little after midnight that there was screaming coming from Madame Toule's house. Luc had stopped by the station on his way home from *La Fleurette* when he saw Matteo leaving to go to the scene.

Ten minutes later they found the front door open of Madame Toule's house and Madame Toule face down in her living room. She was wearing a nightgown but at first glance didn't appear to have been sexually assaulted. The bruises around her neck made it clear enough how she'd died.

Terrified and gasping for her last breath.

"We'll have trouble getting her to the morgue," Matteo said, shaking his head as he observed the body. Luc bit back his response. Madame Toule was overweight, yes. But she wasn't circus lady fat. There was no need for unkindness.

"Check outside," Luc said brusquely as he knelt by the body. "Find the neighbor who reported the screaming."

As citizens no longer had working telephones in Chabanel, all crimes had to be reported in person to the *police municipale*. While this tended to keep the reporting of the frivolous crimes down, it did make it difficult when help was truly needed, especially in the middle of the night.

Luc pulled on gloves and gently touched Madame Toule's head, shifting it from side to side. The body was still warm. He looked around to see if anything in the room had been disturbed but while the place hadn't been tossed, he didn't know what it looked like before to know if anything was missing.

The dark bruises on her throat made it clear the killer hadn't used a rope or cord to murder her.

So, a man.

He stood up. But why? He could see Madame Toule's purse on the table by the front door. He went to it and saw there was money in it.

So, not robbery.

A piece of cardboard had been put in the window. Was that the result of an accident? He would have to check with Eloise to see if Madame Toule had reported an act of vandalism recently.

He glanced back at the body.

Because she was not terribly old, Pauline Toule wasn't on the village list as those vulnerable people needing special care and assistance. He knew she'd retired from teaching a few years earlier. He knew that Jules had been taking language lessons from her.

He turned on his flashlight to look at the carpet but could see no mud or dirt or anything that would reveal tracks of Madame Toule's murderer.

Matteo stood in the front doorway. Behind him Luc could see several neighbors peeking around him.

"Chief?"

"Go ahead and secure the scene," Luc said, frowning at

the gathered group. "Then send someone back to take pictures and move the body."

"I think you're going to want to lock the door and let me go arrest the killer," Mateo said smugly.

"What are you talking about?"

Mateo gestured behind him.

"I've got three people here who all say they heard Madame Toule screaming for her life to someone named *Thibault*."

I couldn't believe what I was hearing.

Murder?

A sudden thought came to me: *the rock thrown through her window*! Did the rock-thrower come back to finish the job?

Just as I was trying to put it all together in my head Thibault's pal Diego roared up the gravel circular drive, spraying pebbles in the air and spooking the poor donkey who was saved from tearing down the road—*les soeurs'* blackberry wine bottles flying behind him—by the quick thinking of Monsieur Augustin who lunged for the donkey's bridle and was only dragged the length of half a football field before being able to stop him.

"*C'est un désastre!*" Monsieur Augustin howled as he glared at Diego who sat in the car oblivious to the mayhem he'd nearly caused.

"You're early," I said to Diego.

I know I've slammed poor Thibault for being a slob but Diego takes the category to a whole new level. You know Pigpen in the Charlie Brown cartoon? Diego was like that only with *major* additional aromas.

Reluctant to get into the car with him just yet—I hadn't even packed!—I decided I could at least use him to help me run my errands before heading to Marseille. I turned to Madame Becque because clearly even Madame Toule's murder wasn't saving me from Madame C's continued pique with me.

"I'll come by the market to say goodbye properly," I said to her.

Madame B nodded and then turned to walk with Madame C to the donkey cart.

I turned to Diego. "Can you give me a lift to the police station?"

He grimaced. "If I must."

Luc stood at the window of the interrogation room in the police station. It was only eight in the morning. On more than one occasion he'd marveled at what a pretty view the room had of the main street and the square *de la maire.* Chabanel's most popular watering hole, Bar á GoGo was visible from this window. Luc could see the proprietor, Romain Armand, placing the bistro tables out onto the sidewalk, getting ready for the breakfast crowd.

"You must know I did not do this," Thibault said woefully.

Matteo had brought him in an hour earlier. Thibault was unshaven and unwashed but Luc wasn't entirely sure that wasn't his normal condition.

Now Thibault sat at the table in the middle of the room, his head in his hands. Eloise had brought him coffee and a croissant from Café Sucre. Both sat untouched.

"I know I need more than you claiming you did not do it," Luc said.

If Luc had any kind of policeman's intuition at all he would swear that Thibault could not have killed that old woman. Unfortunately, the evidence suggested otherwise.

"Where did you go after you left *La Fleurette*?" Luc asked.

Just saying the words *La Fleurette* reminded Luc of last night. Of Jules.

Jules. Who was leaving Chabanel this morning. For good.

"I told you," Thibault said. "I went to the pasture at the corner of the D7 and Monsieur Leboeuff's farm."

"In the middle of the night? Alone? Why in the world would you do that?"

"I wasn't supposed to be alone. I told you. I was meeting someone."

"Who?"

Thibault groaned. "I can't tell you."

"This isn't a game, Thibault," Luc said angrily. "I can't just let you off because we're friends."

"We're friends?" Thibault lifted his head and looked at Luc in surprise.

It was true that Luc had rarely spoken to Thibault before Jules latched onto him but in the months that he'd known Thibault since then Luc had found the man big hearted, even tempered and amazingly honest.

Again, Luc's gut told him there was no way Thibault could be guilty of this crime.

But his gut was not admissible in a court of law.

Madame Gavin poised in the door with a sheet of paper in her hands. "Chief?"

Luc followed her out into the hall. He left the door open and Thibault resumed his earlier position with his head in his hands.

Luc took the report and scanned it as he walked down the hall to his office. His observations were now typed up in the case file.

Pauline Toule was strangled in her home on September tenth roughly between four in the afternoon—when she was last seen —and midnight when her screams were heard by three neighbors. Their names are listed at the end of this report.

As the name Thibault was heard shouted out by Madame Toule at the time of the murder, Thibault Theroux was brought in for questioning.

Now is when you wished you had a little DNA to back up your suspicions, Luc thought sadly. Instead all he had was circumstantial evidence, hearsay and unreliable eyewitness testimony.

Was it still eyewitness testimony if nobody actually saw anything?

He heard a sudden commotion coming from behind him in the direction of the interrogation room.

Would the man be mad enough to attempt to escape police custody?

Drawing his weapon, Luc ran back down the hall toward where he'd left Thibault.

6

TIME'S UP

"What in the world were you thinking?" I
shrieked. "*Who* goes to a field in the middle of
the night?"

I leaned across the table but Thibault refused to lift his
head. It was all I could do not to grab him by his long hair
and force him to look at me.

"Thibault! I'm talking to you!"

When I'd asked Diego to drive me to the police station it
was basically to tell Luc what had happened at Madame
Toule's the day before and then to say goodbye. I have to say
I'd hoped he would be so distracted by the murder that our
farewells wouldn't be massively uncomfortable for either
of us.

I know, I know. I felt bad finding a silver lining in
Madame Toule's early and violent departure from life but
honestly a distraction of this caliber was just what the
doctor ordered.

This doctor anyway.

So imagine my surprise when I got to the station and

Eloise told me they were holding Thibault for Madame Toule's murder!

Well, you don't have to imagine it because I'll tell you. I flipped out.

Who could possibly believe *Thibault* could commit murder?

And right on the tail of that thought, it came to me: Had Luc really arrested Thibault last night after sharing a bottle of rosé with him and commenting on how the grape harvest must be soon and agreeing with him how *les soeurs* had done such a fine job with the garden?

After all *that*, had Luc turned around and clapped poor Thibault in irons?

Well, okay not irons because as I could see Thibault was sitting at a table drinking coffee with a sweet roll but still, *it wasn't good*!

And yes, I admit once Eloise told me what was happening I freaked out and raced down the hall until I found Thibault chained to the...uh, I mean drinking coffee and looking *really* sad...and then of course I lit into him.

All of which put me in no mood to have someone pull a gun on me just when I was trying to sort out a dilemma that never should have happened in the first place!

I looked away from Thibault just in time to see Luc who had materialized in the doorway *reholstering his gun*.

"How in the world did you get in here?" Luc growled.

"You can't question him without an attorney present," I said huffily.

"Jules, *go outside. This minute*," Luc said, his face flushed with agitation. I could see Eloise behind him, her eyes big. She was probably going to be in major trouble for having told me about Thibault.

Trust me, nobody was in a bigger hurry than I was. I had

a certified whacko outside keeping the car running and a boat ready to head out to open sea with or without me and neither was going to wait for me.

I turned back to Thibault. "Just tell me what you were doing in a stupid field in the middle of the night!"

"I'm sorry," Thibault said, shaking his head. "On penalty of my life, I will not say."

"Oh for crying out loud. You're not Patrick Henry! You need an alibi!"

"Well, I don't have one."

I wanted to throttle him! Why was he not trying to help himself?

I turned to Luc. "He was with me last night."

"No, he wasn't," Luc said sternly. "He left *La Fleurette* before I did."

"Yes, and then he came back. I'll swear to it."

"And I swear I'll lock you up right next to him if you lie to me again."

"Jules, don't," Thibault said forlornly. "You'll miss your boat. I have no idea when another chance will come for you to go back home."

"I can't leave you like this!"

Now Luc was moving closer to me as if he might be thinking of physically removing me. My heart beat a little faster and I'm not completely sure whether it was in fear or pleasant anticipation.

"He'll get a fair trial," Luc said between gritted teeth. "He does not need *you* to save him. If he's innocent, it will be revealed."

I really wanted to believe that. I really wanted to go catch that boat back to my real life.

"Are you sure?"

"Jules, *go*," Thibault said. "I'll be fine. It'll all get sorted out. It is just a misunderstanding."

"*Mon Dieu!*" Luc burst out. He grabbed me by the arm and began pulling me toward the door. "Don't think so highly of yourself that we will all just fall apart without you. Catch your damn boat and go back to your own damn country."

I shook loose and ran back to Thibault and gave him a hug and two kisses. Then I walked out the door, past Luc, tossing my hair in as imperious a manner as I could muster.

So much for our big goodbye.

Detective Adrien Matteo would have preferred to break down the miscreant's front door but since he had the door key—confiscated from the suspect that morning—he would have to be content with merely searching the murderer's domicile in the name of justice.

Accompanied by Romeo Remey, the old fart who should have stayed retired and useless from a far but who, thanks to the EMP, had found a second career back at the *municipale*, Matteo had no doubt they would find evidence that irrevocably linked Theroux to the heinous crime he had committed.

He sent Remey into the kitchen, assuming that was the least likely place to find anything incriminating and he himself went straight to the suspect's bedroom. He went through Theroux's dresser and closets, tossing the clothes and drawer contents on the floor.

Annoyingly, he found no weapons or evidence that might connect Theroux to the dead teacher. After scouring the bathroom and not finding even an aspirin to hold against the man, Matteo turned his attention to the living room.

The coffee table was loaded with a pile of dismantled radios that looked as if Theroux had been attempting to repair. Matteo sorted through the screw drivers and utility knives amid the junk, then dragged a large box from the foyer and scraped all the contents of the tabletop into it.

This would be a good job for Eloise, he thought. *She could spend her evenings sorting through this rubbish.*

He stood in the living room tapping his foot, trying to imagine where to look next, when Remey came out of the kitchen.

Already Matteo had processed three rooms in the time it had taken the old duffer to work one room!

"I found this," Remey said. He held out a coffee mug. It took every ounce of Matteo's willpower not to slap it from the old man's hand.

What nonsense was this? Did the old fool think a souvenir mug was valuable?

He was about to say exactly that when he got a better look at the coffee mug. He took it from Remey's hand.

His heart began to race as he stared at the mug.

This was it. The nail in Theroux's coffin. The piece of evidence that would send him to the gallows.

It was a coffee mug with lipstick on the rim. And the words *Teacher of the Year, Madame Toule* in large red letters on the side.

7

OUT OF THE FRYING PAN

Luc watched Jules drive away. A part of him couldn't believe it was over just like that. She'd wanted to go home more than anything else and now she was going.

He felt a sudden difficulty swallowing.

That's all we meant to her? A four-month enforced holiday and then gone? He knew he shouldn't blame her. How would *he* feel if *he'd* been stranded outside his own country? Would he not leap at the chance to return to France?

Even if it meant losing someone he'd started to care about?

No, no, he told himself. *If it were me I would find a way to return and take her with me.*

But that was idiotic. There was no way Jules would have been able to convince me to leave and go with her even if she'd asked. *Why would I think it would work the other way around?*

"Chief?" Eloise stuck her head in the doorway. "Adrien's back. He found something."

It took Luc a minute to remember that Matteo had been searching Thibault's apartment. He frowned.

"Where is he?"

"Right here, Chief," Matteo said, striding into the room and pushing Eloise out of his way. He held up a clear bag as if it were a trophy.

"What did you find?" Luc took the bag and answered his own question. It was a coffee mug with the victim's name on it.

"We need to establish the last time this was at Madame Toule's house," Luc said.

"Already on it," Matteo said. "One of the witnesses in the waiting room said she remembered seeing it at Madame Toule's as recently as this week."

"You already showed someone the mug?"

Luc felt a flash of resentment. This mug was damning evidence against Thibault. If you added to it the fact that Thibault's name had been heard being shouted by the victim at the time of the attack, plus that Thibault had no alibi, and that Thibault had been one of Madame Toule's students during "the bad year"—the year she was accused of sexual misconduct with a minor—it all added up to a seriously air-tight case against Thibault.

He handed the mug back to Matteo and watched the man preen with delight as he left the room to enter the mug into evidence.

I told Jules not to worry, Luc thought, his eyes straying back to the window where he'd last seen her.

I told her all would be well.

He felt a heavy leaden mass settle in his stomach as he thought of the pleasant night he and Thibault and Jules had shared just last night.

And then he thought of how Jules had left his office thinking Thibault would be fine.

And now Thibault was now far from fine.

Katrine jerked the cord on the blind on the living room window and took a perverse pleasure in watching the shade ratchet up noisily, startling her husband where he'd been napping on the couch.

"What the—?!" Gaultier said, lurching to his feet and looking around as if expecting an attack of some kind.

"You said you would watch the girls," Katrine said. "And I've had to hand them off to my mother *again*."

Gaultier looked like a big sleepy bear trying to wake up and for a moment, just a moment, Katrine felt a twinge of irrational affection for her husband. Her irritation at seeing him napping when he'd promised he'd babysit was beginning to fade.

And she didn't want it to fade!

"I am sorry, *chérie*," Gaultier said, rubbing a large hand across his face. "I fell asleep."

"What if I said that to *you*, eh?" Katrine said, feeling her anger fuel a burst of energy in her. "What if I said, *oh, I can't stand six hours in the sun and sell cheese because I'm going to take a nap?* What would you say to that?"

He grinned and when she saw the look in his eye—one she'd seen many times before—she turned to dart away. But she was not fast enough. He grabbed her by the arm, making her squeal, and pulled her to him. With his other arm he hoisted her up into his arms and kissed her neck.

"Gaultier, stop it!" Katrine said, but she was already laughing.

"Do you really want me to stop, *chérie*?" Gaultier said, nuzzling her neck.

"I want you to stop falling asleep," she said, trying to maintain her annoyance with him.

A losing battle as always when he touched her.

"I can promise you I am wide awake *now*, *chérie*," he said in that low velvety voice of his that always made Katrine want to melt into him and forget everything else about her life.

I'm not sure how long I agonized about it. Maybe in my heart of hearts I knew right from the get-go what I'd do. Maybe I knew as soon as I heard that Thibault was in trouble.

But whenever the knowledge came to me, the fact was I knew I wouldn't be going home to the US and all the emotional back and forth seesawing I was doing was just me trying to convince myself that it could somehow still work out.

As Diego drove me away from the police station, my vision was blurred by tears. And the hell of it was I was sure that Luc was right and I didn't need to stay at all! I was absolutely sure it would all get sorted out—with no help from me—and if I stayed I'd only be giving up my chance to go home.

Cue the seething resentment.

"You have no baggage?" Diego asked, looking at my legs.

"Trust me, I do," I muttered. "Can you drop me off at *rue de la Maire*?"

"Eh? We are needing to leave immediately for Marseille."

God, don't make me say it.

"I'm not going. Just drive me up there on the left and then one block."

"You are giving up your seat on the boat?"

The universe is just not going to make this easy on me, is it?

"Looks like it," I said.

There was no way I could take the chance—not even the iota of a possibility that Thibault would get hung for this. I don't know how many friends he has but clearly not many if at least half of them just arrested him for murder.

I trusted that Luc's heart was in the right place but I knew that stretched resources wouldn't allow him to do the work necessary to prove Thibault's innocence.

That would be *my* job.

I hadn't been in post-apocalyptic France for all that long but even I knew that in lieu of forensic evidence circumstantial evidence was now considered good enough to sentence an innocent man to twenty years at hard labor.

Or worse.

Bottom line: while Thibault was being held for a murder I knew he didn't commit I couldn't leave.

Dammit.

"Right here," I said, swinging open my door before the car had even stopped. "Sorry for the wasted trip."

Diego reached out and grabbed my arm before I could get out of the car. He pulled me toward him and planted the most disgusting, slobbery excuse for a kiss on the lower part of my face I'd ever experienced. I yelped, jumped out the car and wiped the considerable layer of saliva from my chin with the back of my hand.

"*Now* the trip she is not wasted!" he said with a laugh as I slammed the car door.

Welcome to effin' France, I thought angrily to myself. All acts of self-sacrifice will now be rewarded in any number of amusing ways—from cretinous sloppy mouth kisses to passing up once-in-a-lifetime opportunities to go back to my home country.

Still shaking with fury and disgust, I made my way to the Chabanel market.

The big market day was every Thursday—like in most villages around this area of Provence—but Wednesdays weren't too shabby. As soon as I got to the small cobblestone square where the market was held I saw Katrine and her husband busily waiting on a group of people. I waved to her as I passed and couldn't help but notice a bruise on her arm. But when she looked at me, her eyes were bright and her cheeks flushed. I saw Gaultier wink at her and she grinned at him.

Whoa! I guess hot married sex does exist.

I was glad Katrine had obviously had a better night than she'd anticipated.

I caught sight of Jim Anderson, the other American expat in Chabanel, who was standing at the roasted nut stand manned by none other than Juliette Bombre. Juliette was the village sexpot and young enough to almost pull it off. I usually saw her simpering around Luc and so basically hated her but now that I saw her pour on the charm with Jim it made me feel a little better.

Jim paid for his nuts and turned to catch up with me.

"Hey, have you heard about Thibault?" he said.

"Yeah, it's just a big misunderstanding," I assured him. "But listen, I know of a boat leaving for the US in about ninety minutes if you're interested."

"Why would I be interested? Not all of us are in France because we're stranded here."

His remark annoyed me. Big time. But I let it go. It's part

of my new self-improvement plan that I don't respond to every mindless quip and incivility I hear. So far, letting this one go was a first for me. So I felt mildly proud of myself.

"A simple *no thanks* would've sufficed," I said tartly.

Okay, so much for my resolution.

Before Jim could respond I spotted the Madame Twins and their booth of bad blackberry wine. I hurriedly waved him goodbye.

"Gotta run! Come by for dinner some time!" I called over my shoulder.

The twins were placing their mismatched bottles of blackberry wine on the wooden table at their kiosk. Seeing them from a distance made me pause. Madame B looked so much younger than her twin but both were concentrating on exact product placement and I have to say it reminded me that this so-called apocalypse had actually given new life to the old girls.

Before the EMP had taken away all our electronics, electricity and cars the two of them had just sat in their apartment and talked to their cat. Now they were making wine, creating inventory chains, interacting with middlemen and engaging customers. They were alive again.

I walked over to their wine stand just as Katrine broke away from her cheese booth and met me there. We kissed in greeting and I confirmed my original judgment that she'd had a pleasant night last night with Hubby. She was still smiling.

"Are you here to help *les soeurs* with their wine sales?" Katrine asked.

"Not if I can help it," I said. "Thibault has been arrested for murder."

"*Vraiment?*" Katrine said with a gasp.

"Totally *vraiment*," I said grimly.

Madame Cazaly looked up, spotted me, and said something loudly and obviously snarky to Madame Becque who also looked at me.

"What did she say?" I asked Katrine as we walked up to their wine booth.

"She said she knew you wouldn't leave."

I'll be damned. I looked at Madame C with complete astonishment. First, how did she know I wasn't here to say goodbye? And second, if she knew I wasn't going, what was all that cold-shoulder drama this morning?

I shook my head at Madame C but she just smiled smugly and continued to set out wine bottles.

Madame B came to me and gave me a hug, her face wreathed in delight.

I still hadn't confirmed that I was staying and couldn't believe the two of them somehow knew I was! Madame B rattled off something to Katrine who turned to me.

"She said she knew you would not leave a friend in need."

Yeah well, I'm glad *she* knew it, I thought with annoyance. *Because as far as I was concerned, I'd been halfway on the boat back to the States.*

"Why did they think you were leaving?" Katrine asked.

"Because I nearly was. Thibault found me a spot on a boat heading back to the US."

"Oh."

"Don't say it like that," I said with rising irritation. "I was going to say goodbye to you and besides you'd have done the same in my shoes."

"Like a shot," Katrine said.

I looked at her and while last night's connubial glow was still in evidence, it was also clear that the main problem, whatever it was, was also still there.

"Can you please tell the old bats that I need them to tell me everything they know about Madame Toule?"

Katrine slapped a hand to her mouth in horror. "Oh, *mais non*! Was it Madame Toule who was killed?"

"Yes, and I need the facts—not the TMZ version," I said pointedly to her. "Gossip and hearsay won't cut it. Ask them what Madame Toule's big-ass secret was. But don't put it like that. You wouldn't know it, but they can be remarkably sensitive."

I noticed that Madame C was watching me carefully. She knew I wanted information on Madame Toule. And I knew she didn't want to give it.

Katrine spoke to the sisters, both of whom looked at each other and shrugged and shook their heads as if they didn't understand her. When Katrine turned back to me I put a hand up to stop her from speaking.

"Never mind," I said. "I get it. They have no idea about any secret. Ask them if they know of any reason why someone might heave a rock through Madame Toule's front window?"

Katrine asked them and while that seemed to shock them a bit, it still did not get them spilling any secrets.

"And while you're at it," I said in frustration, "please ask them if they're okay with Thibault being hung for Madame Toule's murder because *they* are being absolutely *no* help at all."

When Katrine told them, Madame C spoke sharply to her and raised an eyebrow at me as Katrine translated.

"Madame Cazaly said if Thibault is innocent she's sure you will prove it without having to drag poor Madame Toule's name through the mud."

How irritating is it to be complimented and stonewalled at the same time?

"Fine," I said in frustration. "Well, I'm headed back to the police station to tell Luc about the rock-throwing incident which I think I forgot to mention to him earlier."

Madame Cazaly spoke again and then turned away to get more wine from the now donkey-less donkey cart.

"What did she say?" I asked Katrine as she and I walked away from the stand.

"She said next time don't scare her like that."

Unbelievable!

8

ASHES TO ASHES

The minute I split from Katrine and headed toward the police station I realized I was actually closer to Thibault's apartment than the station. While I had no idea what I might find there it seemed like it was worth the time to run over and look around. Who knows? I might find a love note from Thibault's mystery woman asking to meet him in the middle of the field at midnight.

It sounded unlikely but this was Thibault we were talking about. Everything the man did started with unlikely. Besides, if he was thick-headed enough not to help himself when his life was on the line I would feel no guilt about ransacking the place to find clues or information that might help him.

Thibault's apartment was slightly off the center of the village and reachable by a dizzying labyrinth of back alleys and mews. I'd only been there a few times—mostly when Thibault used his ham radio to get in contact with the States on my behalf—and after those few visits had solemnly sworn we'd both be better served by meeting at my place in future.

Not that his place was a dump or anything.

To call it that would be glorifying dumps.

I turned down the final switchback of the cobblestone alley. The last rain we'd had was still evident in the crevice of trickling water between my feet. As soon as I emerged from the alley, I stopped abruptly.

Thibault's front door—a dark wooden affair embedded in a frame of limestone—was festooned in yellow police tape.

I don't know why I thought the cops wouldn't search Thibault's place. He was their main suspect so of course they'd search it. I swallowed my disappointment and continued toward the apartment. After all, the police were looking for things to *incriminate* Thibault.

I was looking for things to prove his innocence.

Relieved that Chabanel didn't have the resources to post a guard by the apartment, I hurried across the street and pulled out my key. Thibault had given it to me the week before so I could drop off some of *les soeurs'* strawberry jam.

I slipped it into the lock, looked both ways down the street, and unlocked the door.

The minute I entered I saw there was no point in staying. I could see from the door that the living room had been turned upside down.

This is Matteo's work, I thought angrily. He had no respect for anyone or anything. Why did Luc keep him on? But I knew why. Nowadays, the police were short-handed. Even toxic, officious little twerps were better than nothing.

I surveyed the mess and realized my trying to search the place was pointless. Anything the cops had found that might help Thibault had already been found and collected —or destroyed. With a sinking heart, I closed the door and stepped back into the street.

As I rerouted my steps in the direction of the police station all I could think of was, *they've already decided he's guilty.*

Luc eased the gear into fourth and sped up to eighty kilometers an hour. He was heading to Nice for an area meeting of all the police. There'd been yet another string of murders in the last day—all on the ring road black market outside Nice.

Something had to be done. They had to come together to find the answer to this. It wasn't just Nice's problem. It was all of their problem.

The DN7 was of course deserted. They'd had to haul stalled vehicles off the highways for months—most of them stripped and useless. It would be many months if not years before any new cars were shipped to the continent. From where?

Germany had been hit as badly as France, their car manufacturing plants as crippled as anyone's. Luc remembered back to the evening at *La Fleurette* when Thibault said that the US was climbing back to its feet at triple the rate anyone might have expected.

Luc had no doubt *their* car manufacturing plants were back in production. The question was, how long until the boats brought the new American cars to Europe? And at what cost?

Most of his countrymen tended to think that since the US was suspected as being the trigger for the EMP they should have the biggest role in reconstruction of Europe. Not surprising for that powerful country, the US had different ideas.

Oh, Luc was sure the US would help. When it was

convenient. And when France was able to pay. Perhaps he was being too cynical. Life was not that much less enjoyable now. He had very few complaints on that score.

Jules was so very American. To Luc she embodied all the best—and worst—qualities of that country. She was independent, she was courageous, she was fresh and original but she would always chart her own course.

Which of course was the problem.

Why had he allowed her to leave Chabanel? How could it have taken him so long to realize that allowing her to decide this step for herself was not in her best interest? He was the chief of police in Chabanel! He could have stopped her. He should have stopped her.

But he had not wanted to appear selfish or brutish and for that vanity he had condemned Jules to a terrible fate. What had he been thinking?

A boat trip from Marseilles? She'd be on the auction block in Bahrain by tomorrow evening!

He reduced speed and eyed the upcoming exit on the highway.

Was it too late to stop her? Would she be in Marseille by now? On board the boat? He noticed the sun at midpoint in the sky and he knew the answer to that. Thibault had said the boat would leave the harbor by midday.

She was gone.

He let the horror and the dread of that knowledge infuse him and he quickly rerouted his thoughts. There was nothing he could do now for Jules. He must focus on what was still in his power. He thought of Thibault and the evidence that Matteo had compiled against him.

In his gut, Luc believed Thibault could not have done this terrible thing. But the evidence, as Matteo was only too quick to point out, said otherwise.

And it all seemed to be piling up at once.

Luc felt a fatalistic dread sink into him once more. Everything was slipping out of his hands.

He had let Jules go when he should have forbade it. He was sitting back and watching Matteo build his case like he had a personal grudge against a good if hapless man when Luc should be energetically proving Thibault's innocence.

The fact was Luc was failing on just about every point there was to be measured.

9

A WING AND A PRAYER

Weirdly, I have to say the *police municipale* in Chabanel is one of the prettiest buildings in the village. A two-story golden limestone building with burnt orange roof tiles and dark green shutters on the three windows on the second story and also on the two floor to ceiling windows on the first floor. The double front door was made of glossy ebony with a French flag hanging over it and at the moment rocking a glowing halo of light around it created by the midmorning sun.

It was interesting to think that this building had been the police station for so many generations. French police chiefs had worked out of this building to solve crimes in Chabanel since the seventeen hundreds. And now that we don't have electricity, electronics or basic communication devices any more, the building actually seemed to make even more sense than it had before—as though it was coming back into its own somehow.

Luc and his staff used a borrowed Peugeot that was usually parked out front. The fact that it was gone, combined with the fact that I could see Luc's pain-in-the-butt second-in-command, Detective Matteo through the first floor window, made me think Luc might not be in the office.

That was fine with me. I'd leave him a message about the rock-throwing incident and if he wanted to talk to me about it, he knew where to find me. Plus, the fact that Luc wasn't here meant I could talk to Thibault more, maybe even wheedle the truth out of him about where he was last night or who he was supposed to be meeting.

I walked into the station and immediately looked around for Eloise. She wasn't crazy about me—probably had a thing for Luc—but she was a mountainside better than Matteo who usually did everything he could to block whatever it was I was trying to do.

Unfortunately, aside from the octogenarian secretary who sat at the high front desk, the only other police-type person in the room was Detective Matteo.

"*Puis-je vous aider?*" the secretary asked me without looking up. I glanced at the full waiting room of grumpy villagers.

"I'd like to speak with Thibault Theroux," I said in clearly enunciated English. "Thibault Theroux," I repeated slowly.

Instantly, douchebag Matteo—yes, I demoted him as soon as I saw him—came to stand by the secretary and took it upon himself to answer for her.

"He is no longer here," he said.

No longer here? Is that why the car was gone? Had Luc taken Thibault some place?

I craned my neck to look down the hall where I'd last seen Thibault as if I might catch a glimpse of him.

"I don't believe you," I said because honestly I didn't know what else to say. I really didn't want to accept that

Thibault wasn't here. I mean, I just left him here not one hour ago! Had they found something when they searched his apartment that put the nail in his coffin for good?

"That matters not to me," Matteo said, openly ogling me and making me very sorry I'd decided to wear my shortest Marc Jacobs skirt which really was too short for anything but sitting on a stool in a dark bar.

"We are busy. Get out," he said brusquely.

Was he serious? I felt my body tensing although some part of my brain did register that I had merely gotten an answer I didn't like whereas these other people probably had real complaints or problems.

But still. *Get out?* Can he really throw me out of a police station? Me, a taxpaying citizen? Okay, well, fine, I don't pay taxes.

But still!

"I'm not leaving until I see Thibault Theroux. Or speak to Chief DeBray."

Matteo took a step toward me and I hate myself for the fact that I took an immediate step backward when he did. I'd never gotten close enough to him to see how he smelled and I didn't want to start a new habit now. Besides, he was looking at me in a way that should definitely have been a crime if only I could come up with the name of it.

Aggressive lookery?

Mentally undressing me without my permission?

He ran a tongue over his teeth—in itself one of the more revolting mannerisms I'd ever been forced to see—and leaned in close.

"Your ability to speak to Chief DeBray when you are upright is not my concern," he said. "Now get out before I lock you up."

I staggered backwards, glancing at the secretary who'd

never diverted her attention from her typewriter and probably didn't understand what Matteo had said to me anyway.

It wasn't until I was outside on the street, my heart pounding with uncontained fury, that I realized Matteo had just implied *to my face* that my usual mode of speaking to Chief Luc DeBray was from a *prone* position.

Katrine stood at the market cheese stand and watched as the people milled through the market. She tried to imagine what their lives were like.

Were they happy? Were they just struggling through? Had they made bad decisions they were now being forced to live with?

She thought of Jules. Stranded in a foreign country but still basically cheerful about it all.

Is that because she lives in hope that her life will change some day? That she'll be able to go back home? Or that she'll find her Prince Charming? Or because she's American?

Every American Katrine had ever met had seemed pretty damn jolly. Or rich. Or both.

How could Jules throw away her opportunity to go home —for happiness? For what? For a friend she'd only known a few months? Was this Jules' secret to being happy? Putting others before herself?

If that's the case then I should be delirious with joy since everyone's pleasure and needs come before mine.

Gaultier paused in his wrapping of a particularly challengingly shaped *reblochon*.

"Are you okay, *chérie*?" he asked, his brow puckered in concern.

Perhaps it is not doing those things that are expected of you, she thought. *Not accommodating your husband and children, your parents or even the poor. Perhaps Jules' secret knowledge is that she knows that the more she gives the more will come back to her.*

It couldn't hurt to try.

"I am just restless. You will be fine alone here?"

Gaultier looked surprised. "Of course."

"I will pick up the children when I'm done with my errand."

"No, I will pick them up, *chérie,*" Gaultier said firmly, and Katrine felt a flush of gratitude and then immediately scolded herself for feeling it.

He is not doing you a favor!

But in spite of knowing that, she still felt a little better.

I had more or less stopped fuming by the time Katrine found me with the first of my two free cocktails of the day at the Bar á GoGo.

The guy who runs the place, Romain Armand, is pretty dishy I have to say. About my age, no ring on his finger— which honestly doesn't mean much in France—and very attentive in a non creepy way—which means he pays attention to me without staring at my boobs all the time.

I was delighted to see Katrine because she was usually not free to get together twice in two days. The cheese-selling business must be very demanding. Plus the whole kids and husband thing. I honestly don't know how she does it.

"Jules!" Katrine called to me from the outdoor portion of Romain's bar. "I thought I'd find you here."

We air-kissed and while she ordered her drink I took a

moment to worry about what it meant that she expected to find me in a bar in the middle of the day.

"How did Gaultier let you off the leash?" I said as Romain brought a dish of olives to our table.

"Gaultier does not have me on any leash," Katrine sniffed. "Quite the contrary, I assure you. I told him I had something important to do."

"You seem a little more relaxed today."

Katrine sighed and turned her face to the sun. I could see she was struggling with her emotions and I realized I'd been too quick to think a roll in the matrimonial hay had solved whatever she was struggling with.

"There's just so much to do all of the time," she said finally. "The kids, the cheese stand..."

"Gaultier pitches in, doesn't he?" I asked.

Katrine rolled her eyes.

"If he watches the kids for me it's like he's doing me a favor. I have to remind him they're *his* kids too."

"Sounds like he's pretty traditional."

"He is a man. He thinks childcare is my job."

"Along with selling cheese and keeping house?"

"Pretty much."

"Remind me not to marry a Frenchman."

Katrine looked and me and smiled wanly. "Any risk of that?"

I put my hand on hers and squeezed it.

"Hey, I know things are getting up your nose these days, Katrine," I said, hoping she understood the idiom, "but Gaultier is a good guy."

"I know," she said as Romain brought her a glass of sherry.

"So what was this important thing you told him you had to do?"

She looked at me in surprise.

"Why, I am here to help you prove that poor Thibault is innocent, of course. Or did you think you could do that on your own?"

I grinned at her. It looked like her midlife crisis had a definite upside to it, at least for me. All kidding aside, I really appreciated her help. Hey, she was the Beth to my Nancy Drew!

"So how do we start?" she asked.

"Well, first we need to put together a list of all the people who hated Madame Toule."

Katrine frowned. "Nobody hated Madame Toule."

"Well, clearly *someone* did, because she ended up murdered. Second, we need to talk to the parents of the child she was messing around with."

"The 'child' will be in his thirties by now," Katrine said. "Why not just talk to him?"

"Well, okay," I thought, a little peeved that "Beth" seemed to be grabbing the reins from "Nancy." *Katrine does know the role of sidekick, doesn't she?*

"So, we need to know his identity," I said.

Katrine pulled a ballpoint pen out of her pocket and held it poised over one of the Bar á GoGo's cocktail napkins. "How do we find that out?"

"We talk to people who were either in the same class with Madame Toule or anyone who might remember her from that time."

"Like *les soeurs*?"

"As I'm sure I don't need to remind you," I said, "as far as spilling Madame Toule's secrets *les soeurs* are being less than helpful at the moment."

"What about the crime scene? Don't we need to get access to it or see the report on it?"

I guess *Law and Order* reruns were a thing in France too before the lights went out.

"I don't think that's likely," I said.

"Can't you use your special relationship with Luc DeBray to get the information?"

"I'm not sure how *special* that relationship is any more," I said, wincing as I remembered how he practically threw me out of the police station that morning.

"Well, it was bound to change I guess when he moved on."

"What do you mean *moved on*?" All of a sudden I was very awake and whatever buzz I'd been working from my lone glass of *kir* evaporated in the time it took Katrine to say the words *moved on*.

"I thought you knew."

"Knew *what*, Katrine?" I felt a prickling on my scalp as I waited for her answer.

"Juliette Bombre was bragging at the *boulangerie* this morning about how she and Luc are together now."

10

END OVER END

Well, that would certainly explain why Luc hadn't made his move yet.

After Katrine and I split up, I went to what served as the city hall of Chabanel. The mayor's office was in the same building—again, a very attractive, very old limestone building with dark green shutters with the ubiquitous flower boxes crammed full of geraniums in every window.

At one time Luc had hinted that Mayor Beaufait was possibly not my biggest fan and while I was pretty sure I could win her over once she got to know me, Luc asked me to avoid her if at all possible.

Luc. What's his deal, anyway? Arresting Thibault when he knows Thibault couldn't possibly have hurt old Madame Toule! *And dating Juliette?* Really? *She's* his type? Well, so much for any mystique he might have had because as far as I'm concerned, a guy who was into Juliette Bombre was about as obvious as you could get.

I told myself I'd simply been wrong about Luc and as that had happened to me a time or two in the past with other men, I wasn't exactly gasping with astonishment that it had happened again.

Still. It had taken me off-guard.

Fine, I thought. I hope the two of them will be very happy. Her with her pointy bouncy girls and her too-short skirts, and him with his sexy grin and full lips. Oh, crap. Clearly I just needed to move on, myself.

I pushed thoughts of Luc and Juliette out of my head— as much as was humanly possible while still keeping my head attached to my shoulders—and went up the smooth stone steps of the town hall determined to think only of Pauline Toule and whatever secrets public records might reveal

An hour later I was back outside and walking to the nearest *boulangerie*.

There's something about coming up short in every other department in life that just makes me hungry. I refuse to think of it as stress-eating. Rather, I think of it more like filling a void with something tasty and buttery and full of sugar because *why not*?

The good news about my hour spent talking to the very gregarious secretary in the records department, Madame Lidou, was that I'd actually found someone who knew the name of the boy Pauline Toule had slept with as well as the file on him and his whole family.

The bad news was that everything I found out led to a complete dead end and as soon as I stopped thinking about Pauline Toule and her past indiscretions or Thibault's chances of escaping the guillotine, visions of Luc and Juliette locked in a passionate embrace came roaring back to my mind.

Like many people before me I have found in these situations that a fresh *profiterole* or chocolate *éclair* is often the solution. It doesn't get me any closer to the truth, but it still chalks up a mark in the positive column of an otherwise frustrating afternoon.

I bought my *éclair* and settled down on the nearest bench I could find to enjoy it. Unfortunately, that enjoyment was pocked with very real concerns that I was not going to be able to help Thibault after all.

The records I found at the city hall revealed that the boy in question, one Romain Toulouse, and his family had moved from Chabanel soon after the incident. Even if I found someone to interrogate about the details of all that, I still didn't know French well enough to form the questions. Or understand the answers.

I ate my *éclair* as I tried to think of my next move. I did also discover that Toule was Pauline's married name which I found interesting. Was she married at the time of the incident? Did her husband divorce her as a result of it?

Madame Lidou said while she had no definitive record to support it she seemed to remember Madame Toule's husband had also left the village at about the same time as the Toulouses.

But why? And to where?

Oh, to have Google for just five short minutes!

Maybe Madame Toule's husband came back—finally ready for vengeance on being made a fool of—and finished her off?

It had been twenty-two years since the scandal of Madame Toule and the student. If that incident was the reason for her murder, twenty-two years was a seriously long time to wait for payback.

~

Luc watched the man who believed Luc had humiliated him among his peers last summer. Achiles Sommet, Brigadier in Aix, had barely retained his rank after last month's embarrassment involving several Americans and the murder of one of the most celebrated pastry chefs in all of France.

Luc knew Sommet had every reason to hate him but today they'd been asked to put aside all petty politics and personal feelings in order to tackle this common problem of the Nice "special" market together. Luc nodded at Sommet as he entered the conference room but wasn't surprised when the man only lifted the corner of his lip in response.

Beyond Sommet, Luc could see the heads of most of the law enforcement agencies in Provence, from Nice to Nimes and south to Marseille.

He took his seat and instantly began tapping his fingers on his knee. The time he'd taken to come here was precious and he would be missed in Chabanel.

He nodded his greeting to his superior, Jean-Paul Tourner who stood alone, scanning the room of policemen. For once the man showed no levity. The fact was every man in this room was in the same situation. The Brigadier-Chef Principal David Coste had not brought them here to waste their time.

Coste, a burly man who strained the seams of his uniform with his obvious appreciation of good food, was a decent sort if somewhat severe.

The problem of the Nice "special" market was his but if it wasn't stopped, it would be all of theirs very soon. There wasn't a man in this room who didn't know that.

"Thank you for coming," Coste said. "We'll get right to it so you can return to your districts."

Coste stood at the front of the room of fifteen fellow officers, his face creased with stress and gloom.

There had been three murders since Monday and another two yesterday. As Luc was coming into the room he'd heard that there was another one last night.

"Every man in this room knows the problem we are facing," Coste said. "A special transit black market on the ring road around Nice appears to be operated by the lowest elements of the criminal sect."

"Are we talking refugees?" one officer called out. Luc recognized him as Michel Lestrange, Bridgadier in Avignon.

"No," Coste said. "I mean thugs—the basest stratum of society from every country bordering France as well as within our borders. There is no common denominator that sets these criminals apart except their desire to make money and create mayhem. Some are mafia from Italy. Some are ex-cons from Syria. But they are all here for this special market."

"How have they organized? How is that possible?"

"Unknown at this point," Coste said briskly. "There are hints that it sprang from the human trafficking markets outside France. There are reports that the women being sold at the Nice special market come from outside France and are then taken back outside France."

"What about the murders?" Luc said, raising his hand. "Who is killing whom?"

Coste looked flustered.

"The murders are Niçoise citizens who go to the market to take advantage of the reach and special deals offered at the market," he said.

"How long has it been going on?" another man asked.

"Six months," Coste said. "Up to now, the bastards were only killing each other."

And you didn't care then, Luc thought.

"Now the murders are happening two, three a night. Some are obvious executions, others theft-related."

"What do you need from us?"

"One man from every district," Coste said. He lifted his hands immediately. "I know, I know! We are all short-staffed! But if we don't stop it in Nice, it will soon spread to the rest of Provence. We must stop it now before it can infect the rest of our country."

There was a silence as everyone digested the Brigadier-Chef Principal's words.

Luc exchanged a glance with Jean-Paul. The look he received was resigned but determined. They would do what was necessary regardless of the cost at the village level.

"I'll need your commitment before you leave today," Coste said. "Today it is voluntary. In two weeks it won't be and I will remember the ones who didn't raise their hands."

Nice threat from the head boss, Luc thought. But he agreed with him. If Coste felt more manpower could stop this infection from spreading to the rest of Provence, then Luc would gladly hobble along even more short-handed than he already was in Chabanel.

For a moment, Luc thought of Thibault and wondered how much *he* knew about this market. It definitely sounded like something right up Thibault's alley. In the meantime, Luc would make an official proclamation warning the citizens of Chabanel not to go—in fact he'd make it easy on them and make it a crime to travel to Nice for the next six weeks.

Neat and tidy.

Jules would be appalled.

His heart clenched at the thought of her and where she might be at this moment.

And he hated himself—truly hated himself to the point where he wasn't sure he could ever forgive himself—because of that careless, human moment when he hadn't acted in time to save her from whatever it was he knew she was enduring at this very moment.

11

LIKE TWO SHIPS

I finished the last bite of my chocolate éclair and daintily wiped my fingers on a paper napkin. It was a lovely day, the sky so blue it hurt your eyes to see it, a gentle breeze ruffling my long hair and caressing my bare arms. I'd optimistically worn a cotton eyelet sleeveless top with a linen mini skirt, thinking if I willed it to still be summer and dressed the part, Mother Nature would comply. So far it was working.

I think I would probably still be sitting on that bench with a lap full of pastry flakes if Jim Anderson hadn't strolled up to snap me out of my trance.

He'd just come from the *boulangerie* himself which gave me a chance to apologize for my snarky comment to him this morning.

Unlike how most places operate in most restaurants of the world Café Sucre was okay with customers bringing their own donuts and croissants as long as they bought their coffee at the café.

I'm kidding. Where are you going to find *donuts* in the south of France?

Anyway once we moved to the café, I had Jim's complete attention to hear my very sincere apology which he met with a tight smile and a hearty "no problem!" which only meant he'd been nursing hurt feelings all morning.

What a lot of work men are, am I right?

Honestly, I can't tell you for sure what my relationship with Jim is because I do not know myself. At one point a few months back I thought he was coming on to me and while I wasn't against the idea I did think he was hurting my chances of getting together with Luc which—at one time in history—I had some wild idea might actually happen.

But now, I just don't know. I've had gay guy friends in the past but can't really say I've ever had a guy friend who didn't at least on some level want to sleep with me. I know that sounds conceited but I'm afraid I'm going to have to stand by it.

It doesn't mean they want to marry me, but they'll hit it and risk not being able to have coffee with me later.

Jim was not only good looking, smart, American like me which these days counted double bonus points, but he was not totally clueless about women—something not a lot of guys are.

Hello, Luc?

As soon as we started talking about Thibault and poor Madame Toule, the clearer I started to see certain points in the case.

You know how some people can just bring that out in you? Even if they don't provide a lot in the way of specific ideas themselves, they somehow help spur your brain to go places you wouldn't have gone without them?

That's what talking to Jim was like. To a private detective, this reflective idea-bouncing capability of his was extremely helpful.

"I just don't know why the cops are so hell bent on proving that Thibault killed her," I said.

"Why are you so sure he didn't?" Jim asked.

"You don't know Thibault like I do. He wouldn't do it."

"If you say so. But there must be evidence or they wouldn't have arrested him."

"You know how the French are always saying *cherchez la femme*?"

Jim frowned. "You think Thibault and Madame Toule were..."

"No, Jim," I said patiently. "I'm pointing out the obvious fact that there is no real *femme* here to *cherchez*. Don't you see? The cops are pinning this on Thibault for lack of anyone better. But imagine who there *might* be if Thibault *wasn't* in the picture."

"I have no idea."

"Exactly. That's because Madame Toule was a virtual hermit. She'd stopped teaching ten years ago and hardly ever went out of her house. Have you heard the rumors?"

"About her and one of her students? Everyone has."

"Well, did you know she was married?"

"Are you sure?"

"That's what Madame Lidou told me this morning at the Chabanel records department, except there's no paper trail of what happened to him."

"I think the village records went digital with all that stuff about ten years ago," Jim said. "Too bad."

"So the information exists," I said. "Just no place we can access it."

"There should still be a record of it at the paper."

"What do you mean?"

"The paper was digital, of course, but it also relied on

microfiche files for the longest time. Seems the old editor was averse to the new technology."

I felt an excited breathlessness infuse me.

"Do you think you can get a hold of those microfiche files?"

"I think so. I've been working a lot with Esteban recently. What do you want to know?"

"Madame Toule's husband's name. What happened to him. When did they divorce, if they did. And if he's still alive, where is he?"

Jim wadded up the paper pastry bag and tossed it in the air like a ball.

"You got it," he said.

I went into the evening at *La Fleurette* in a much better mood than when I'd left. While it was true I had no more information than I'd had then, I felt like I had allies. Both Jim and Katrine were interested in helping me so even without any viable clues or leads, I felt like at least now I'd made progress.

Unfortunately, I imagine poor Thibault would need a little more than that to feel the same. Had they really moved him out of Chabanel? Why? To where?

Les soeurs were already home by the time I arrived. They were busy slicing tomatoes, grinding fresh *herbes de Provence*, and cutting creamy goat cheese into fat cubes to be tossed with the salad.

We all had high hopes for the garden that the sisters were planning for the spring—a long nine months away at this point—but the *potager* hadn't been in too bad a shape when we moved in to *La Fleurette* so we always had fresh rosemary and parsley. And in France, that is no small thing.

As usual, I could only understand the barest gist of what the twins were saying but they were able to pantomime pretty effectively that they'd sold all their wine at the market for either money or favors.

Which explained the lovely plate of lamb chops waiting to go on the grill. I didn't feel all that sociable with the old biddies seeing how at least one of them had been a complete witch to me this morning and neither of them would give me the information I needed to help Thibault.

Speaking of Thibault, soon after we'd moved into *La Fleurette*, he'd set up a shower system for us inside the house that enabled me to have a daily shower without needing to haul buckets from the creek. As if.

After a day like today—mostly frustrating and underscored by the loss of my one chance to return home—I figured I'd could splurge with a second shower.

It had been a warm day but as fall crept ever closer, I knew the evening would be coolish. What I didn't know and couldn't help but wonder was whether or not Luc would show up tonight.

After all, him coming to dinner at *La Fleurette* obviously had nothing to do with the two of us since it seemed he'd been dating someone else all along anyway.

But our last interaction had been a volatile one and except for a brief mad moment in Aix last month where I accused him of trying to get rid of me and siding with the police in an anti-American campaign, it had been the most upsetting incident between us yet.

Was he mad at me? Did he think I was mad at him?

Well, honestly, I *was* mad at him!

Which didn't mean I didn't want to see him.

After showering and dressing in jeans and a cotton sweatshirt, I came outside to the terrace to see that the table had been set for four. So either the old ladies knew something I didn't or they too were assuming Luc would be here tonight.

Cocoa ran up to me and gave me the kind of greeting I am now thoroughly accustomed to getting. I knelt to nuzzle her and she licked my face.

"I could never have you left you, girl," I murmured to her. Having once more established her undying love for me, she darted away after the same invisible squirrel or vol in the garden and I was left alone in the garden with my thoughts.

I noticed a glass of rosé had been poured for me and left by my place in a sort of peace offering and I felt a stirring of guilt for being such a pill with *les soeurs* when I came home. They were only doing what they thought was right. It wasn't their fault if they gave me more credit than I deserved as far as being able to free Thibault without knowing what they knew.

Madame C was bustling around the kitchen while Madame B was working on getting the grill hot. Since they were both in such great moods I forced myself to soften enough to let them know I was glad their wine—their truly terrible wine—had sold well today.

"*Salut*, Justine," I said to Madame B, lifting my wine glass up and watching to see if the calling-her-by-her-first-name thing was going to stick.

But she was clearly too happy with the outcome of her day to notice. After she got the fire going, she came over to me and patted me on the knee.

Her eyes were bright and inquisitive.

"What's up?" I asked, taking a large swallow of the wine

to fortify me. She and Madame C didn't often ask me to do things for them but when they did it was usually either impossible or illegal or both.

"*Du vin*, she sell *bien aujordhui*," Madame B said.

"Congratulations," I said, warily, waiting for the other Birkenstock to drop.

"*Une grand marché à Nice demain*," she said slowly, watching my eyes to see if I was understanding.

"There's a big market in Nice tomorrow," I said dutifully.

"Very good, Jules!" She clapped her hands.

"Why are you telling me this?" I asked politely, hoping to hurry this process along.

That she did not understand but it didn't seem to matter.

"*Thibault allait prendre notre vin sur le marché.*"

"Something about Thibault and your wine and the Nice market," I said. "Wait a minute. Did you arrange for Thibault to take your wine to Nice tomorrow?"

She nodded energetically, a smile breaking open across her face.

"*Oui*, Jules!"

"Okay, so you know he's otherwise engaged tomorrow, right?" I said, narrowing my eyes.

She pointed at me.

"You, Jules. *You* take wine to Nice."

And there it was.

Only about a hundred things flitted through my mind as I watched Madame B as she waited for my answer. But the only thing that mattered was that she wanted something from me and I wanted something from her.

"Me no got car," I said in French.

"Thibault car."

That is true. Thibault had a car and I knew where he kept his spare set of car keys. If the cops hadn't found them.

"Okay," I said, pointing to myself. "Me take wine to Nice."

She smiled and stood up. I grabbed her hand.

"But you will tell me what I want to know."

She frowned and pretended not to understand me. I waved a finger at her.

"I know you know what I'm saying. Thibault needs my help. I gave up a trip home to help him. A chance to see my mother, my condo, my friends. I gave all of it up to help him and *you* are going to help me do that."

She smiled faintly. I'm sure she didn't understand a word I said but I was equally sure she got the crux of it.

I noticed Madame B's hands were flecked with blue paint. I knew she'd intended to spend the morning painting a pair of broken down garden chairs. I hoped that at least some of the paint had ended up on them.

"Tell me Madame Toule's secret," I said.

She said a bunch of French but her face didn't look like she was revealing a secret. It looked like she was giving an excuse for why she wouldn't.

I crossed my arms on my chest in my best international pictogram of stubbornness.

"If you want me to take your wine to Nice, you need to tell me her secret."

She watched me for a moment, her smile now gone, and then turned and walked back into the house no doubt to confer with Madame C.

I wasn't sure how I felt. On the one hand, I was delighted to have some kind of bargaining chip to finally crowbar the info out of the old biddies.

On the other hand, Nice was a four-hour drive by car. And frankly, I'd heard a few scary stories about this particular market. Nothing too concrete. Just enough to make me uneasy.

If I remembered correctly the Nice market was every Thursday, which was tomorrow.

I leaned back in the chair and looked at the sky and felt the warmth of the day's sun still in the cushions of the patio furniture. I sipped my wine and tried to let the events of the day—and my insecurity over what was happening to Thibault—ease out of me. I closed my eyes and when I opened them, both Madame Becque and Madame Cazaly were on the terrace with me.

"We tell you," Madame B said, her face serious.

Before I could leap up and fist-pump the air, I heard the sound of the garden gate opening and turned in time to see Luc DeBray walk into the garden.

12

ANY PORT IN A STORM

L uc had not seen that outfit on Jules before. The jeans were snug and clung to her every curve. If he were closer, he was sure the color would match perfectly her flashing eyes.

Because make no mistake they were flashing.

Seconds after stepping foot in the office he'd been informed that Jules Hooker had not left Chabanel after all. He'd been relieved that it was Eloise who'd told him and not Matteo because he was sure the look of flushed delight on his face upon hearing the news would *not* have been something he would have liked Matteo to have over him.

It was all he could do to wait for evening before rushing over to *La Fleurette* to see with his own eyes that Jules had in fact stayed in Chabanel.

And now here she was. Not on a boat headed to the slave markets of Abu Dhabi or even to the golden sands of Miami Beach, but right here in her own back garden, a glass of wine in one hand, her dog scampering about her feet and surrounded by the people who love her.

"So," Jules said, arching an eyebrow higher than one

might think humanly possible, "are you here to help me prove Thibault's innocence or fuss at me again?"

"Last time I heard you were on your way to Miami," Luc said dryly, thoroughly enjoying the pleasure of sparring with her once more. Madame Becque handed him a glass of wine.

"Don't remind me," Jules said, then turned away to watch as Madame Cazaly placed several pieces of seasoned lamb on the grill.

The sound of the sizzling meat combined with the fragrance of grilling herbs that Madame C had sprinkled over them instantly made Luc's mouth water.

The table was set for four so, as usual, *les soeurs* knew what he hadn't—that they'd expected Luc to come. He found their assumption exceedingly reassuring.

"It turns out you're just in time," Jules said, handing him a plate of sliced tomatoes, so red and ripe their juices pooled on the dish.

"Ah, yes?"

"The Madame Twins were just about to lay on me a major development in our murder case. You can translate for me."

Luc bit back his first response to the reference to "our murder case" because he didn't want to do anything to make Jules regret having given up her chance to go back to the States. While he was sure there was nothing she could do for poor Thibault—the man was determined to hang himself—the last thing Luc wanted to do was make Jules think her sacrifice had been for nothing.

Madame C spoke to Luc and he turned back to Jules.

"Madame Cazaly said if you could be so kind as to wait until dessert and coffee," he said.

"Fine. Just as long as they know neither of them is leaving this garden without telling me what they know."

"I'll refrain from translating threats if you don't mind," Luc said with a wry smile.

"In the meantime, you can tell me what *you* know."

He'd come to dinner tonight fully prepared to. Once he knew Jules hadn't left the country after all, he was frankly surprised at how accommodating he was prepared to be. He was *that* relieved.

"Ask me what you want to know," he said, knowing *les soeurs* couldn't understand English and so would likely not be upset by anything he told Jules.

"How did Madame Toule die?"

"She was strangled."

Jules paused as if digesting this. "So a woman couldn't have done it?" she asked.

"We don't believe that's likely, no."

"And why did you decide Thibault was your guy?"

"The neighbors reported hearing Madame Toule scream out his name."

"Really?"

"Over and over. Three neighbors. There can be no mistake."

"Thibault is an unusual name."

"It is. And there is only one in Chabanel."

"When was she killed?"

"Midnight."

"And Thibault's apartment? What did you find there?"

Luc hesitated. The souvenir mug was the so-called nail in the coffin for Thibault. It was the one thing that couldn't be talked around or explained. It was concrete evidence.

Luc found he didn't have the stomach to tell Jules that.

"Nothing much," he said.

It's a strange sensation being attracted to someone and also wanting to punch him in the face. I can't say I've felt it too often. Every time Luc laughed his golden rumble of a laugh —the one that made me feel all squishy inside and want to peel grapes for him—I remembered that Juliette and he were doing all manner of unspeakable things on a nightly basis and that she of the cheap-o fingernail art and post-apocalyptic hair extensions was his preferred companion.

Cue the urge to want to punch him.

Why was he here anyway? Why was he laughing and pouring wine and chuckling with the Madame Twins as if he was a part of the family when his hottie was waiting for him somewhere back in whatever shoddy paramour's love nest they hooked up in?

Oh, it all just made me so mad!

To avoid looking like I gave two craps *what* he did with his free time or with whom, I forced myself to focus on what he was telling me.

First, whoa! Strangled? Poor Madame T! Secondly, why would the neighbors all say they heard her screaming Thibault's name? That made no sense at all. I made a mental note to see if Katrine could get free tomorrow to go knocking on doors with me.

I was relieved about them not finding anything at Thibault's apartment. As it was we were only looking at circumstantial evidence—and not much of that. I was feeling much better about Thibault's chances. Luc must be too, I thought, because he looked positively gleeful.

Although that was probably due to thoughts of his late-night booty call with Juliette.

I spent the next several minutes clearing away the dishes

and bringing out coffee cups and the strawberry tart that Madame B had made. This tart was one of her specialties although everything she made was worthy of being showcased in a high-end *pâtisserie*.

The one thing you can say about strawberries in Provence is that they aren't just pretty but really *taste* like strawberries. I didn't love the extra time it took these days to whip the cream by hand but I agreed with Madame C that we couldn't serve the tart without fresh whipped cream.

By the time we got the table cleared and reset to look like something Martha Stewart would weep for joy to behold, it was totally dark. Luc lit the two big lanterns we kept at the end of the patio and Cocoa curled up under the table in her dog bed—one of many—where she would be in prime position for any bits of crust tossed her way.

I poured the coffee and passed the whipped cream as Madame B cut big wedges of tart and handed them out.

This is how I know the whole ritualistic eating thing in France will live on no matter how many dirty bombs get dropped on us—hey, notice I said *us*?—because when it comes to sharing food there's a reason we pause, refresh, sit back and enjoy ourselves. I honestly don't know what that reason is, possibly it changes every day or something, but I do know there's a reason because it all just feels so right.

I'm not going to say I'd forgotten that the sisters had promised to come clean with their big secret but I was having a very special moment with Madame B's strawberry tart and was surprised when Madame C cleared her throat and tapped her coffee cup with her spoon, indicating she was ready to begin.

Feeling the anticipation I used to feel before the start of a really good movie, I added a glug of brandy to my coffee, passed the bottle to Luc, and then settled back to hear what they had to say.

And all I can tell you is, oh baby, did they have a story to tell.

"We have known Madame Toule for many years," Luc translated as Madame C spoke. "While not close nor really friends—and there were many reasons for that..."

At this point the two sisters conferred with each other and eventually must have come to the decision that whatever those reasons were they weren't a part of the original agreement with me.

"Anyway," Luc said as Madame C continued, "we were not close but there was mutual respect between us."

The Madame Twins were in their early nineties now and I'd have put Madame Toule at late sixties so there was around a thirty-year age difference. In any case, I reminded myself that they weren't peers and would have few reasons to hang out together.

"In a village the size of Chabanel," Luc said still translating, his voice holding back barely repressed amusement, "it is difficult to keep secrets from your neighbors. Some might say impossible. But Madame Toule's secret was one that was fastidiously kept and guarded."

"Okay, I feel like this is the movie trailer part of the story," I said, making a hand gesture to indicate that Madame C should pick things up. "Tell her I get that it's a big secret. I'm on board. That's why I want to know it."

"I'm not going to tell her that," Luc said. "You'll hurt her feelings."

"Impossible."

Madame C crossed her arms and glared at me, totally getting the gist of my hurry-up motion to her and now refusing to go any further. Madame B picked up the baton.

"It was many years of very strange and sometimes only subtly strange behavior before we were able to realize the secret that Madame Toule guarded so carefully," Luc said.

"Both of you must have been watching too much television," I said. "Just tell me!"

"A secret," Luc intoned, unperturbed by my outburst, "that only a few people would ever learn. Not even Madame Toule's husband knew." Madame B nodded smugly as if she'd just dropped a bombshell.

"Tell her I already know Madame Toule was married," I said. "She'll have to do better than that."

"Well, *I* didn't know it," Luc said, but he translated my words.

Madame C shot off a salvo of words in French—*funny, until I met her I'd always thought French was such a melodic language*—and then recrossed her arms against her chest, her eyes on me in triumph.

Luc's mouth fell open.

"What did she say?" I asked.

But now all three of them were talking, the two old ladies were nodding their heads in confirmation and Luc was not looking even a little bit less astonished the more they talked.

"What are they saying? What are they saying?" I said loudly, prompting Cocoa to jump up and run around the terrace barking as if we might be in the process of being invaded.

"They said," Luc said, shaking his head as if still taking it in, "and if this is true, it definitely puts a whole new light on the murder case..."

"What did they say!?"

"They said that Madame Toule was really a man."

13

TIME AND AGAIN

Katrine wrapped the two wheels of Brie de Meaux, tied them with twine and handed them to Madame Leguere with a brisk, "*Merci*, Madame!" Her back was beginning to ache just a bit but it was nearly five and they'd close the stand for the day soon.

Two more people in line. Katrine glanced over her shoulder to see Gaultier was already beginning to load up their cheese onto the bike cart.

She turned back to smile at the American Jim Anderson who was next in line.

"*Bonjour*, Monsieur Anderson," she said musically. "How can I help you this afternoon?"

"You can help me, Madame Pelletier," Jim said, "by calling me Jim so I can call you Katrine. Please?"

Katrine blushed with pleasure. Jim Anderson was a very handsome man and the flattery of his attention notwithstanding it was never a bad thing for your husband to see that other men found you interesting.

"*Bon*," she said. "Jim. May I interest you in a nice Banon? It is lovely with fruit or all by itself."

"Sounds good," he said. "I'll take two kilos."

Two kilos! That nearly made their week for them. Although she knew Jim Anderson had money—all Americans except Jules had money—Katrine was still pleasantly surprised.

"Heard any good gossip?" Jim asked as Katrine sliced the thick wedges of cheese onto wax paper.

"None that I can tell you," Katrine said with a laugh. "How about you?"

Even before the EMP gossip and village news was valued but now that nobody had access to cellphones, TVs, computers or even radios, news of any kind—anywhere in the world or the country—was a premium.

If somebody was smart, Katrine thought, *they would open up a store and sell news. The line would wrap around the block for that!*

"Not really," Jim said as he watched her carefully wrap up his purchases. "But have you heard about the murders at the Nice market?"

Katrine stopped wrapping.

"Murders?"

"Yeah. Seems there's this special market on the ring road around Nice. I'm surprised you haven't heard of it. Juliette Bombre knew of it."

Katrine felt slightly dizzy as she finished wrapping Jim's cheese but managed to give him a cheery smile as he took it, paid for it and left.

She waited on the rest of the customers as if in a dream. All she could think of was the fact that Gaultier had mentioned this very market to her only this morning, saying that with one visit they could make a month in profits—with only half their cheese.

Did Gaultier know how dangerous this "special" market

was? Had he heard about the murders?

Did Katrine not have enough on her plate without having to worry about this too? She would talk to him as soon as they closed and tell him that he was not going to this market. It didn't matter how much money they made.

Nothing was worth your life.

No matter how desperate you might be.

The next morning I was still trying to process what the sisters had revealed last night and frankly, a part of me just wasn't buying it.

Madame Toule a transvestite? Or did that make her a transsexual? I shook my head at the thought.

Les soeurs seemed to believe Madame Toule hadn't had any surgeries but had lived her years in Chabanel as a man trapped in a woman's body. A very fat woman's body.

But I was well aware that it would be totally like *les soeurs*—especially *Madame C*—to decide that *deal or no deal* they'd stonewall me with a big fib.

When Luc had stopped laughing I could tell he wasn't buying it either. Whether that was because he didn't want to have to rethink his whole murder case or he really thought the sisters were making it up, I don't know.

In any case, we had a very pleasant rest of the night and then he went off to have wild crazy monkey sex with Juliette Bombre. Or whatever.

It was so hard for me to think Luc really did come to *La Fleurette* for a pleasant few hours with me and the old ladies and then turn around and found his girlfriend for a late-night rendezvous.

And yet what other explanation was there for why he hadn't made a move on me yet?

As I was reflecting on this over my morning espresso on the back terrace, Madame C came to the door and cleared her throat. She had her white hair tied back off her face in a worn kerchief and was wearing an old apron or *tablier* over her day dress. She and Madame B had been up early to bottle more blackberry wine to get ready for the special market tonight in Nice. They'd made it clear to me that I shouldn't mention to Luc—or anybody—that I was going to Nice.

They'd also made it clear that the information they'd told me last night about Madame Toule was off-limits for dissemination.

I looked up from my espresso and *pain beurre.* Cocoa stayed pretty close at most meal times but bread and jam was one of her favorites and her chin was virtually glued to my knee. Ghengis Khan himself could come through that door and she wouldn't look away from the prospect of a piece of bread coming her way.

"Monsieur Anderson," Madame C said.

It was unusual for her to announce any of my friends so when I saw the stern arch of her eyebrow, I realized she was making an exception in order to underscore her edict to me about not telling anyone what she'd revealed last night about Madame Toule.

How am I suppose to solve this thing if I can't tell my helpers everything I know?

I tossed a last morsel of bread to Cocoa who caught it in midair. Jim walked onto the patio behind Madame C who gave him an untrusting look—pretty much her standard greeting to everyone.

"You've just missed breakfast," I said. "But there's still coffee."

He sat down and tousled Cocoa's ears.

"Nah, I can't stay. I just wanted to give you what I found yesterday at the paper."

I felt a tremor of excitement.

"You found Madame Toule's missing husband?"

He laid a piece of paper on the table in front of me with a few hand-scrawled notes on it.

"Sorry, no. That was a big fat dead end. But what I did find was a name change application for Gerard Toulouse in Dijon where the family moved to after they left Chabanel."

"They changed their name?"

Jim nodded. "To Armand."

"Wait. The same name as the owner of Bar á GoGo?"

"Exactly."

"So Romain's father changed their family name?"

"Appears so. They moved away for twelve years which is what you discovered when you went to city hall. But they came back and when they did, they were the Armands and nobody ever made the connection."

"The whole family moved back?"

"Just Gerard and the kids. The mother had died of cancer by then. Gerard died not long after they came back."

"Why did they change their name?

Jim shrugged. "Who knows? You could probably ask Romain over at the Bar á GoGo."

"Don't think I won't. How many kids were there?"

"Just Romain and his sister, Juliette."

My eyebrows shot up. "What happened to her?"

"There was no information on her but if you're thinking what I think you are, let me say right now that Juliette is a fairly common name in France."

"So you *don't* think Romain's sister is Juliette Bombre?"

"If she was, why does she have a different last name?"

"Maybe she's just continuing the family tradition of changing her name every couple of years?"

"And maybe you have a reason why you'd like to lay some dirt at her feet?"

I blushed. Wow. I hate being so transparent.

"I am an objective investigator," I said huffily as I brushed breadcrumbs off the table and watched Cocoa try to snap them out of the air.

"Sure you are, Jules," Jim said with a grin.

14

TOO MANY COOKS

T wo hours later I was in place for my stakeout at Romain Armand's Bar á GoGo. It was only eleven in the morning but since I needed a reason to be sitting in Romain's bar, I'd already gone through both my free *kirs*. I was tempted to order lunch but since I wasn't completely sure my work today wasn't going to implicate Romain in a murder, I thought that smacked of conflict of interest.

I watched Romain as he worked the bar. Once in awhile he'd wait on a table but mostly he had a kid named Thierry who did that. Now that I knew Romain was the child Madame Toule supposedly messed around with, I studied him closely to see if he looked mentally deranged or not.

That is a very difficult thing to try to ascertain from a distance—not to mention two drinks in.

The fact that Romain was the kid who had been with Madame Toule wasn't the only thing I was grappling with this morning of course. If the Madame Twins were telling the truth and Madame Toule really had been a man living as a woman all these years in the village then I needed to get my head around how that changed things.

I tried to imagine different scenarios where this information was critical to what happened to her. A few were pretty obvious.

If Madame Toule had made a pass at some guy who then found out she was a dude, that encounter might well end in a two-handed flesh necklace. I frowned. Except it would more likely result in a beating than a strangling. A beating was an angry reaction to something. A strangling was slow and methodical.

A strangling was more in tune with a premeditated murder. Like perhaps a boy who'd had a fling with his older teacher and had his family driven from the village as a result of it? And perhaps if later when he was grown up that boy discovered that his first sexual encounter had been with a man?

Yeah, I was liking this theory.

Well, of course not *liking* it. But it made sense.

I watched Romain and tried to imagine how he'd have felt if he'd somehow discovered that the woman who took his virginity wasn't a woman at all.

But, to be fair, I forced myself to think of other scenarios too.

For example, could Madame Toule have hidden her true sex from the man she was married to? Honestly, I'd heard of things like that happening. Was that a motive? If her husband found out the truth?

I rubbed the chills off my arms. I'm sure some men could kill for much less.

I'd been at the bar nearly two hours before Romain—and even Thierry—started giving me odd looks. Normally I was pretty comfortable hanging out at a café or bar for as long as I liked and never worried about anyone wanting to turn a table. But the Bar á GoGo was getting busier the closer we got to lunch time and all I'd done was take my two free drinks and ask if I could have some complimentary olives.

Since one of the requirements of a stakeout is not to become obvious to your subject, I decided to move on. Besides, I wasn't learning any more about Romain by watching him except possibly that he was probably thinking that the identity of thieving bottle washers was not worth two free daily drinks.

I'd have to find a moment to interview Romain at some point but I was hoping for a little more background information before I did.

And for that, I'd need to go to the guy who'd actually sat next to him in school.

∾

Thibault looked tired and unshaven but still happy to see me.

Luc revealed to me last night that Thibault had *not* in fact been moved from Chabanel. Just another example of that twerp Matteo messing with me.

I didn't see Luc or Matteo on the way into the police station—always a plus—and Eloise said her boss had instructed her to allow me access to Thibault whenever I wanted. So that was cool.

I met with Thibault in a small lounge area, not the interrogation room. He was uncuffed although I noticed that the octogenarian part-timer Romeo Remey stood outside the doorway where he could listen to us.

After Thibault and I greeted each other, I got down to

business.

"Have you told anyone who you were meeting in the pasture that night?" I asked.

"Jules..." he said wearily. "I cannot tell you that."

"Fine." I hadn't really expected him to tell me. It was annoying but like so much in life, I'd already accepted that I was going to have to do this the hard way.

"Did you know that Romain Armand used to be Romain Toulouse?"

"The owner of Bar á GoGo?"

"Yes. He was Romain Toulouse when he was in school with you. You seriously didn't recognize him?"

"I thought he moved away."

"He did. But he moved back."

Thibault shrugged. "We didn't hang out as kids."

"So you don't remember him at all?"

Thibault frowned as if in deep thought.

"His mother," he said.

"Yes?" I prompted. "Romain's mother. What about her?"

"She was a mean bitch. I remember that."

I sighed. "Is there anyone else from your class who might still be in the village?"

Thibault frowned. "Maybe?"

"Okay. You're officially no help."

"Half the time I skipped class. Sorry."

I glanced out the window of the police station. There was a huge plane tree outside losing its leaves. I could see them scattered all along the walkway. Fall would soon be here—crackling fires, walks in the woods, a snap in the air. And it would be really nice if Thibault was able to enjoy it from outside a prison cell.

It occurred to me that I needed to find out who else was in Madame Toule's class in 1998—the fateful year. Perhaps I could go to the village school and get my hands on a class roster? The school was not far from Madame Toule's house and I'd heard it was out of session this week.

I was instantly cheered to have a plan. And breaking into...er, I mean *visiting* the village school...seemed like a good start on one.

"You will tell *les soeurs* I am sorry about missing the market in Nice tonight?" Thibault said sadly.

"They've already found a fill-in," I said.

Thibault shook his head. "No, Jules. It is too dangerous. You must not go."

"It's just a market, isn't it? Selling beads and lavender sachets?"

"It is too dangerous," Thibault repeated sternly and then his face cleared. "Or if you insist, get Diego to take you. I can tell you how to contact him."

Not wanting to tell Thibault that I'd be more afraid of Diego than anyone he was assigned to protect me from, I assured Thibault I'd either contact Diego or I wouldn't go.

I hate to lie to my friends but honestly, has Thibault *met* the old lady twins? Does he even *know* what's involved in saying *no* to them?

I said goodbye to Thibault, encouraged him to keep his chin up, and hurried out of the room and down the hall— thoughts of breaking into the school dominating my thoughts—when I ran smack into none than Juliette Bombre.

Juliette gave a fake little squeal and grabbed the large wicker basket she was carrying as though I might try to snatch it from her.

Her makeup was cheap and garnish, her long talon-like fingernails coated in azure blue with sparkle stars and little crescent moons—so tacky! She must have done them herself. I hadn't seen a nail salon in Chabanel even before the EMP went off.

"Watch yourself!" I said gruffly, although arguably the collision was my fault. I caught a glimpse inside Juliette's basket and saw a carefully wrapped cake, strawberries, and a small tub of whipped cream.

Instantly I felt sick.

It was the cardinal rule of romance in this country and I was an idiot to have forgotten it: For a Frenchman, there could be no more immediate avenue to his heart than food.

Why had I never brought Luc homemade strawberry shortcake? Or a loaf of banana bread?

I hated seeing evidence of Juliette's obvious superiority in these matters. True she was French and so she knew the cultural rules of love innately but that didn't make it any less hard to take.

It's very possible she saw all that registering in my face— her successful checkmate in the romance department— because she instantly smirked when she saw where I was looking.

"*Pas de problème*," she said. "I am half awake today because Luc is keeping me up past my bedtime. You are understanding?" She turned away in order to throw her last line carelessly over her shoulder at me.

"As if sleep has anything to do with it," she said.

Bullseye.

I just hate it when the trailer trash ho gets the last word. Don't you?

15

SOUNDS LIKE A PLAN

Old man Rousseau ran the fish booth at the Chabanel market and was currently leaning against the main pillar that kept Katrine and Gaultier's cheese booth erect. Gaultier had his head down as he listened to the old fellow. Gaultier was always so respectful with the elders in the village.

Katrine smiled fondly at him and tried to imagine that one day Gaultier would be one of the wise ones that the younger men came to listen to. She could definitely see it.

Business was light today probably because yesterday had been decent. Unfortunately, whenever they had a good day of sales Katrine couldn't help imagining that they were on a new business trajectory instead of just one more peak before a dip. It wouldn't matter so much except little Loulou's teacher had told them last week that Loulou really needed glasses to see the board at school. In the old days it would be a simple matter of going to the doctor, paying a nominal fee and waiting for the delivery of the glasses.

But nothing was simple nowadays. They had gotten a prescription for the glasses from the national health system and then Gaultier found a source for the glasses themselves. They cost over a hundred euro. And the retail source was not interested in taking cheese instead of payment.

Just as well. To give away that much cheese would make it impossible for them to break for the month.

Why was there always something to manage? To grapple with? Had life ever been easy? If you have children, was it ever easy?

Gaultier and Monsieur Rousseau came around to the front of the stand. Katrine saw that Gaultier had given the man a sizable package of cheese. She didn't begrudge him that. God knows she'd given away half the store in the first few weeks of knowing Jules.

"*Chérie*?" Gaultier said. "Monsieur Rousseau has an interesting story about a friend of his who—"

"My nephew," Monsieur Rousseau said.

"Yes, well, his nephew, who brought nearly five hundred kilos of *aubergines* to the Nice 'special' market and sold every one for twice what he'd been charging in the villages."

Monsieur Rousseau nodded his head with pride.

"A smart boy, my nephew. He's going back tonight, he said."

"Where does your nephew live?" Katrine asked, not taking her eyes off Gaultier. She could see how excited he was, how much he wanted her to green light this for them.

For the sake of Loulou's glasses.

"He lives in Avignon," Monsieur Rousseau said.

"Ah."

"But if you are interested in going," Rousseau said, "I have heard that *les soeurs* are selling their wine at the market tonight."

Katrine wasn't at all sure she had heard correctly.

"Are you saying...are you sure?" she said, her eyes wide with disbelief.

"I heard it from Madame Cazaly herself." Monsieur Rousseau nodded to Gaultier. "I am sure she would be grateful for another set of hands if you want to go tonight. Well, I am off. *Merci*, Gaultier! *Au revoir*, Madame Pellietier."

Katrine watched the old man toddle off into the sparse market crowd. It had been an hour since anyone had approached the booth and then they'd only wanted a sample.

"Did you hear, *chérie*?" Gaultier said. "His nephew got *twice* his normal price!"

"I heard."

"Imagine if we were to get ahead of things just a little. We could relax. *You* could relax."

I can never relax, Katrine thought, but she looked at her husband and saw the hope in his eyes. She felt a surge of love for him that warred with a mirroring surge of anxiety.

Would he be safe?

The extra money would be so good right now.

And Gaultier was a big man. Surely nobody would mess with him. Surely it would be fine?

Since I was nearer to Thibault's apartment than the village school, I decided to go ahead and pick up the car from his garage and drive it to *La Fleurette* so *les soeurs* could begin loading it with their wine for tonight. I'd walk from there to the school, find the class roster, and be back at *La Fleurette* in time for a bath and a relaxing drink before the old ladies forced me to drive to Nice and the French re-enactment of Mad Max Thunder Dome.

You've heard of best-laid plans? Yeah, that.

As I drove Thibault's old Citroen 2CV rambling wreck down the main street of Chabanel everyone I saw on the street looked up and watched me. As they would. It had been four months since there'd been any motorized vehicular traffic in Chabanel beyond Luc's police car. Even Thibault never drove his car in the village, using it only for trips beyond it boundaries.

While I was trying to put together exactly how I'd approach the school, I drove past the Bar á GoGo and noticed Romain was outside wiping down tables. He looked up as I drove by and on impulse, I slowed and put the car in park.

I think maybe on some level I was thinking if things went sour I could always race away. Which meant I was thinking that things could go sour. I hate when deep down I know how a thing is going to pan out but I go ahead and do it anyway.

The minute I stopped the car, Romain tossed his rag down and walked over to where I was parked. He looked at the car admiringly.

"Is Thibault's, yes?" he said, his eyes glittering with desire. For the car.

"Yep," I said. "He's letting me use it for an errand."

Romain's English wasn't great but it was a hundred times better than my French. I'm not sure how so many people in France learned English as well as they did but I've been grateful for the fact on a daily basis since I landed here.

As I watched him circle the car as if he were about to make me an offer on it, I put my thoughts together and very quickly realized that this was my chance to get some answers from the horse's mouth.

"So you and Thibault were in school together, right?" I said.

Big mistake. As soon as the words were out of my mouth I realized what I'd done. Romain was living under an assumed name. Nobody was supposed to know he'd once lived in Chabanel, let alone went to school here as a child.

I wish I could tell you that Romain was so enamored of the car that he didn't hear or understand me but that is not what happened.

He literally froze in mid stride around the car and then turned slowly to look at me.

"What did you say?"

"What?"

How does a person rewind the tapes and make what had come out of her mouth *not* come out of her mouth?

Romain moved to my driver's side window, his neck corded with his fury.

"Who told you that?" he roared, clenching his fists and unclenching them. "Who told you I was in school here?"

"Well," I said, licking my lips and easing my now shaking foot off the clutch to get ready to speed off. "I just heard that you...your family used to be called *Toulouse*. Is that not so?"

Crap! I was making it worse! I could hear the words coming out of my mouth like projectile vomit and I wish you could have seen the transformation in this man—from confused discomfort to full-on insane mania.

Instead of easing off the clutch my foot jerked and the car stalled. Thibault's car did not have electric windows and there was no way I was going to be able to crank the window up by hand before Romain grabbed me and dragged me through it.

"Who have you been talking to?" he screamed, spittle literally speckling across me and the car door.

"No...nobody," I stuttered as beads of sweat formed on my upper lip. I restarted the car, jammed the clutch in and rammed it into first gear with a horrifying grinding sound. The car lurched forward but thank God did not stall again and I gunned the engine.

In my rear view mirror I saw Romain standing in the street jumping up and down in thwarted fury.

I have no doubt if I hadn't gotten away that he would at the very least have struck me.

At worst, strangled me.

As I drove toward *La Fleurette*, my stomach gurgling painfully as my nerves took full possession of me, my mind was a nauseating whirl of a hundred different thoughts that all centered on the same thing: what *innocent* person behaves like that?

I think I just answered my own question, I thought, clutching the steering wheel in an effort to control my shaking.

By the time I arrived back at *La Fleurette*, I was calm again—or at least calmer—and Romain had definitely moved to the top of my suspects list. I couldn't wait to talk to Luc and tell him what I'd learned.

Thinking of Luc formed a picture in my head of his skeptical face. It was maddening but no matter what great theories I had or perfectly logical sounding suppositions, annoyingly, Luc always wanted *proof*.

Good Lord, I thought as I parked the car in the front drive roundabout. How much easier life would be for all of us if we had proof! I mean, even a school kid could do Luc's job if he had a pocket full of proof!

But still, I knew I'd get nowhere with Luc if I didn't have something besides Romain's bad temper and the fact that he was living a lie.

That meant the visit to the school was on.

I got out of the car and opened the trunk so the sisters would have no trouble loading up their wine. I knew what they *really* wanted was for *me* to load it up but as they weren't out front to see me and as I had a very important errand to run, they'd have to settle for an open trunk lid.

Hurrying in case *les soeurs* came out of the house at any moment, I turned and jogged back to Chabanel.

16

THAT WHICH DOESN'T KILL YOU

"But I am in the middle of an active murder investigation!" Matteo whined. He stood in the center of Luc's office, half his shirt tail out and coffee stains down the front of his chest.

"Most of the work on that has been done," Luc said. "The special Nice market is tonight and you will go this afternoon and report to Brigadier Tourner at eighteen hundred hours. That is all."

Matteo emitted a insubordinate snort and turned on his heel and stormed out of the room. Luc was surprised that the man didn't jump at the chance to take the car. He probably realized he only had enough time to get to Nice by eighteen hundred hours. He would have no time to stop at a bar along the way or enjoy the beach before it was dark.

"And take Theroux with you," Luc called. "He's to be detained at the Nice *municipale* until trial."

Luc was not sure how much help it was to send Matteo to join the forces at Nice but it beat going himself. He'd had a call from Jean-Paul to report that they still had no clue at what point on the ring road the market would be held.

It was amazing to Luc that average citizens in Nice knew this information but the police had not been able to ascertain it. They had a few rumors to go on and the plan now was to set up three or possibly four stakeouts at various spots on the highway and hope one of them would hit pay dirt.

Unfortunately, communications were still so stunted it would be virtually impossible to call in the rest of the forces for a combined show of strength if they *were* to find the market tonight.

Luc found himself smiling at the memory of his evening last night at *La Fleurette*. Everything was so easy and relaxed. Perhaps it was time after all to move things forward with Jules. She *did* give up her opportunity to go back to the States. Perhaps he had judged her too soon about her desire to return to America?

His eyes fell on the remnant of the strawberry cake in the basket on his desk and he felt a mixture of guilt and desire. He'd been a fool to lead Juliette on as he had. Honestly, it had been a low moment last week underscored by his belief that another woman would be a good way to distance his heart from a certain American who was sure to break his heart one way or the other.

But it wasn't fair to Juliette who was definitely acting like the two of them had a real shot at a relationship.

Why do I always make things harder than they need to be?

He stood up and reached for his jacket. He'd stop by her house and thank her personally for the cake. It was too early in the day for her to get any ideas about his visit and it would give him a chance to let her down gently.

"Chief?" Eloise popped her head in the door to his office. "You going somewhere?"

"Why?" he asked.

"Marie Gaston's ten-year-old is caught in a tree in the old Gabort pasture on the west side of town."

Luc snorted in frustration and glanced at his watch.

"Adrien just took off in the car," Eloise said. "And I've got Madame Dernoir in the office right now."

"Madame Dernoir? What's the problem?"

"She's making a formal complaint about her neighbor. Stole her cherry *gateau* recipe or something."

Luc sighed. "Fine," he said. "I'll handle the ten-year-old in the tree."

As he snuffed out the light in the hurricane lamp in his office, his eyes fell on the strawberry cake again.

Juliette would have to wait.

The only reason I can give in my defense as to why I decided not to break into the school after all is that I realized that breaking into a public institution would be much more difficult to explain if I were caught than, say, explaining why I was found wandering through someone's back garden.

Or their living room.

Well, that was part of the reason. The other part was the fact that on my way to the village church I passed Madame Toule's house and it struck me that breaking into her house would be way easier than the school and probably yield the same results.

After all, there was no way someone like Madame Toule wouldn't keep records of all her teaching years at the school and all her students, but *especially* 1998.

As I neared her house I wasn't surprised to see that there wasn't any sign of an ongoing police investigation at the house. After all, it had been nearly two full days. There was no guard posted and no crime scene tape cordoning off the place.

Clearly the Chabanel police had their man and saw no further need to maintain the crime scene.

With no more access to DNA analysis, it was doubtful what good even collecting samples was these days. And when three citizens had all reported hearing your suspect's name screeched out during the middle of said crime, well, why bother processing the scene at all?

I glanced up and down both ends of the street in front of Madame Toule's house. It was totally empty. There was not even a flicker of a curtain in a window to indicate that a nosy neighbor might be watching me.

I ran to the front steps and knelt to find the key under the mat where I knew it would be. I'd seen Madame Toule put the key there a few weeks ago when she'd misplaced her own set.

I let myself into the house and shut the door behind me. The house was even quieter than the street outside, making me think of the ultimate in quiet—a grave. I tried to shake off the image but my skin had already begun to crawl.

There was no way to know where Madame Toule had fallen after being murdered. There was a space in front of the coffee table in the living room that was wide enough— just barely—to hold her bulk spread out and just as I instinctively tried to push that image away too, I reminded myself that envisioning the crime was part of what I needed to do in order to entertain all likely alternative scenarios.

So I imagined poor Madame T sprawled out on her back, her eyes open and glassy staring unseeing to the ceiling while her killer stepped around her.

I took a deep breath to steady my nerves and moved to the opposite wall to Madame Toule's desk. There was a computer on top with a thin layer of dust on its keyboard but nothing much else. If there had been, the police likely had bagged it all up. The computer, of course, was useless. Even if it had important information on it about people Madame Toule may or may not have been in contact with, there was no longer any way to access that information.

I pulled open the top drawer of the desk and saw that the cops had been uninterested in the assortment of pens, pencils, erasures, rubber bands and old batteries that were in there. The other drawers appeared to be just as useless. There was a hole-puncher in one, a paper shredder—also useless nowadays—a battery-operated hand scanner, a few hairbrushes and a small photo album with no photos in it.

I found a few postcards but they had no postal mark on them or any writing leading me to believe that Madame Toule herself had probably bought them. One had a picture of Notre Dame Cathedral on it and the other was of the beach at Nice.

Had she gone to these places on vacation once? Was she alone when she'd gone?

I felt a wave of sadness. Whether Madame Toule was a man or woman, her life had seemed so lonely.

I pulled the handful of pens and pencils out of the first drawer and caught a glimpse of a scrap of newsprint beneath them. I dumped the pens on the desktop and extricated the newspaper clipping.

It was a newspaper clipping from five years ago announcing the opening of Bar á GoGo.

With mounting excitement, I scanned the article and turned the clip over to see the continuation of the piece stapled to the back. The photo showed a headshot of Romain Armand with the caption *Romain Armand recently of Dijon is the owner of the new bar.*

But that wasn't what made me catch my breath.

What made me know I had stumbled onto something big was the fact that someone had taken a pen and vigorously crossed out Romain's face.

As if to obliterate him.

Still waters ran deep, I thought as I walked to the front window to see the clipping in better light.

This was proof that Madame Toule not only knew Romain had come back, but also that she hated him.

But why? Why had she blamed Romain—surely the victim in all this? Maybe it was self-hate turned outward?

As I tried to see how the pieces fit, my eye caught something on the carpet by the coffee table. As I knelt down, I realized this was exactly where I'd knelt two days before when I examined the rock that had been hurled through Madame T's window. I touched the carpet and pulled back my hand. The tips of my fingers had tiny flakes of blue paint on them.

I was still kneeling on the floor staring at my hand when the door burst open and Detective Adrien Matteo strode into the living room, a pair of handcuffs dangling from one hand, and a malicious grin slithering across his ugly face.

17

A DAY LATE

What a little turd.

Detective Matteo indeed. If France wasn't currently so hard up for uniformed manpower, this little pipsqueak would be pumping petrol at the French equivalent of the D7 Jiffy Mart.

While all of that was inarguably true and it did make me feel a little better, unfortunately it didn't change the fact that Detective Matteo had the power to clap handcuffs on me and march me through the streets—making me break a heel in the process!—to the *police municipale* where he unceremoniously handed me over to Eloise Basile for processing.

It seems Madame Toule's street wasn't nearly as vacant as I'd thought. No fewer than four people had personally trotted into the *municipale* to report that Madame Toule's house was being robbed.

Even so, how Matteo thought he would get away with arresting and incarcerating *me*—an American citizen—I have no idea. Plus, I was pretty sure Luc would not allow it.

Not a hundred per cent, mind you, but pretty sure.

Okay, yes, it's true I was trespassing or maybe even

breaking and entering if you want to get technical. Whatever. But I was fully prepared to play my *I'm a hapless foreigner and got lost* card. It was a lame gambit, I'll admit, but that didn't mean it wouldn't work.

When Barney Fife Matteo handed me over to Eloise, I had to admit I expected a much more relaxed reception and thank God, that's exactly what happened. Make no mistake, I *was* officially arrested and if they were starting a file on me in post-apocalyptic France then I had my first entry into it—unless what happened to me last month in Aix counted because I was thrown in jail there too.

In any case, after Eloise did her duty by booking me, she and I found a quiet spot in Luc's office for a cup of coffee. She'd been in the process of enjoying a late lunch and since I couldn't remember the last time I'd eaten and since the State was now responsible for feeding me, we both chowed down on her buttered baguette stuffed with ham, cheese, and tomatoes.

"The Chief will be furious," Eloise said as she cut the sandwich in half and handed one half to me. I reminded myself that I'd gotten her in trouble with Luc only yesterday and she was probably not eager to repeat the experience.

I just as quickly reminded myself that I was doing all this for Thibault—to prove his innocence. A little collateral damage along the way was to be expected.

"How is Thibault?" I asked.

Eloise shrugged and also shook her head. This is a neat trick if you've never seen it before and one every French person masters in nursery school. I've seen the French do it in response from everything as serious as a dead body to a forgotten manicure appointment.

"It is so sad," she said. "Everyone likes Thibault."

"Well, it's not over yet," I reminded her. "I'm working on finding evidence to help clear him."

"Is too late, I am being afraid," she said.

"Too late?" *Unless that idiot confessed or something, it was never too late.*

"The evidence found in his apartment, yes? The coffee mug with Madame Toule's name on it? You are knowing? The chief said he briefed you."

I stared at her, the hand with the sandwich, frozen halfway to my mouth.

"He did brief me," I said slowly.

Eloise nodded. "So how else can such a thing be interpreted?"

Luc lied to me? The thought wouldn't gel at first but it quickly took root. I felt my anger bubble over. He withheld information from me which is the same as lying. They *did* find something in Thibault's house!

"How would *you* interpret it?" I asked, cagily.

"To have found a coffee mug with Madame Toule's name on it? A mug that three neighbors have sworn they saw her use just days before her murder? Is very bad for him."

Crap. How could they have found that in Thibault's house? How in the world did he come to have such a thing?

Could it have been planted by the police?

I would not put it past that weasel Matteo. He'd made the collar and now he was going to make sure it stuck.

But could even that little worm do something so low? To steal something from the crime scene and plant it at the suspect's house to seal the deal?

My mind was whirling with questions and possibilities.

And all along Luc knew this and didn't tell me?

I heard steps coming from outside in the hall and from the volume and force of them, I could tell they were angry and they were coming toward us. Eloise must have thought so too, because her eyes got big and she jumped up, grabbing the sandwich wrappers from our lunch as if to attempting to hide all evidence of our having eaten it.

Luc burst into his office, the door crashing into the wall behind it. A framed picture fell to the floor, its glass shattering.

He looked at me, his eyes snapping with fury.

"I do not believe this," he said in English. Without taking his eyes off me, he snarled something in French to Eloise who scurried from the room.

"If you'll let me explain," I said. But although I definitely felt like the wronged party in this little scenario I have to tell you the sight of a six foot three man vibrating in anger does a little something to the average person's composure.

"Explain what? How you broke into Madame Toule's house? How you violated an active crime scene—"

"There was no yellow tape."

"Do not even think to argue with me about this!" Luc bellowed.

Well, gosh. How was I going to explain my side of things if I'm not allowed to argue with him?

Luc came into his office and walked to his desk and then walked back again. He was clearly pacing and for a moment I thought he might put his fist through one of the walls.

If the wall hadn't been made of stone two feet thick.

I dearly hoped he wouldn't try.

He was obviously trying to get a hold of himself and it suddenly occurred to me that perhaps an offense was my best defense.

Note to my future self: no. Just no.

"You lied to me about not finding anything at Thibault's house," I said.

His mouth dropped open at my accusation. If the desk hadn't been between us, I think he might have lunged at me, I kid you not.

"You said you didn't find anything!" I said.

Luc made a successful and very visible effort to calm himself. When he spoke again, his voice was lower and his tone guarded.

"The evidence that was found in Thibault's house—" he began.

"...is bullshit!" I interrupted. "You found a mug that belonged to Madame Toule? That makes no sense. Why would the real killer keep that? He would be implicating himself!"

Luc took in a long breath and spoke evenly. "It's called a souvenir."

"And he'd just leave it out in the open? Are you blind? It was planted!"

"That's crazy. Who would go to the trouble?"

"Besides the police? How about the real killer?"

Luc's eyes narrowed and I could see he was back to barely being able to control himself. I'm pretty sure it was that crack about the police having planted evidence.

"You are very close to adding more charges to the original one," he said, his eyes flat, his teeth gritted.

"Thibault was lured to that pasture *deliberately*," I said, ignoring Luc's threat. "Don't you see? It was to make sure he didn't have an alibi."

"You are giving the killer too much credit."

"So you don't think this was premeditated?"

"Of course not."

Talking about the details of the case seemed to force Luc to click back into police robot mode and out of impassioned crazed guy mode. I made a mental note to always try to throw facts at him in future when things got too hot between us.

"This was an act of fury," he said.

"I disagree. Fury is when you pick up the lamp or the nearest thing to you and start battering to death the object of your annoyance. This was not fury. This was an *execution*."

"Then why not use a weapon if it was premeditated?"

"What better murder weapon is there in a time with no forensic science than your own two hands? You don't have to worry about fibers or hairs or prints or blood droplets or anything! And you don't have to worry about trying to dispose of the murder weapon either because it's attached to your arms!"

"This conversation is idiotic."

Well, that wasn't very nice! I couldn't believe Luc wouldn't listen to me. I couldn't believe he would discount the possibility of Thibault's innocence just because of a stupid coffee mug!

"I can't tell you how tired I am of you saying that to me when someone's life is hanging in the balance," I said.

"And I can't tell you how tired I am of finding you behind bars! I'm a policeman! You do see that, yes?"

"I see a man who's so hamstrung by rules and assumptions that he's blind to the facts when they're staring him in the face. That's what I see."

"Is that truly what you see?"

We were both furious and I realized right about then that we both needed to shut up about five minutes ago. I turned and faced the wall, my hands on it, feeling its hardness, hoping we were done being horrible to each other.

"How can I let you off with a warning?" he said in a quiet voice.

"Don't bother. In fact, while you're at it, why don't you reinstate whipping posts? I'll bet you'd love that!"

"France never had such barbary. You are thinking of your own country."

"Oh, right because *you* only cut off people's heads!"

I was pretty happy with having the last word—and let's face it, it was a doozy—but less so with the fact that it prompted Luc to storm out of the office, slamming the door behind him.

And even less when seconds later none other than that douchebag Matteo came in with a triumphant grin on his face to make sure I knew that he'd overheard every word of my conversation with Luc.

"Speaking of the guillotine," Matteo said, his hands resting on his plump hips, "I thought you might be interested to know that it has been reinstated in *la belle France*—and for crimes much less serious than what your friend Monsieur Theroux is charged with."

I was so shocked at this news that I just stood there and stared at him which effectively allowed the little bastard to get the last word on *me*.

18

SHE'S GOT GAME

After Matteo left, Eloise came back and silently led me to the front waiting room. I sat there while a few villagers came in with their grievances and while Eloise dealt with them. I didn't see Luc or Matteo again.

Surely that nonsense about the guillotine was just Matteo trying to get a rise out of me? I had to believe it was a lie. It just had to be.

Finally, the door opened and to my complete shock Madame Cazaly came in, looked around and then, spotting me, began to nod her head as if she'd just won a bet or something. She interrupted poor Eloise who was in the middle of dealing with a very irate woman and began speaking to her in fast, clipped French.

It was amazing to see how everyone in Chabanel stepped aside where the sisters were concerned—but especially Madame C. Whatever the two of them had gone through during the war—and there was really only rumors at this point—they had forever bought themselves positions of respect and reverence.

Eloise nodded her head at me and Madame C turned to leave but not before arching that famous eyebrow at me. I got up and followed her out.

I shouldn't have been surprised that one of the twins came looking for me. After all, the Nice market was tonight and they would be understandably uneasy about where their driver was. But I was falling down shocked when, once we'd left the *police municipale* Madame C led me across the street and down another one to the Café Sucre.

In the whole time I'd known either of the Madame Twins, we'd never eaten at a restaurant or gone to a café together. So when Madame C—thin as a rag and dressed in all black—pushed her way through the late afternoon crowd into the café, well let's just say I wasn't the only one with her mouth open.

The owner of the café, Theo Bardot, rushed over to take our orders. Theo was about fifty years old so he'd grown up with *les soeurs* in the village. They were the stuff of legends. And clearly Monsieur Bardot had heard and believed all of them.

Even though we were nowhere near the main drag, I still felt it necessary to look over my shoulder for Romain. I couldn't imagine he'd forget about me—or what I'd revealed I knew. The question was, *what would he do about it?*

And would he do it with the level of agitation and frothing at the mouth that I'd witnessed this afternoon?

"*Madame Toule devrait pouvoir se reposer maintenant,*" Madame Cazaly said softly.

I had no clue what that meant. On impulse, I pulled the news clipping that I'd found at Madame Toule's house and laid it in front of Madame C.

She frowned when she saw it and I thought I saw a nerve

twitch in her cheek. I spoke very slowly and hoped she'd get most of what I said.

"Madame Toule knew that the kid she was accused of molesting was Romain Armand," I said.

She looked uncomfortable.

I pointed to the scratched out photo of Romain Armand. "This looks like she was *très colère* ...very angry with him. *D'accord?*"

She tore her eyes from the clipping and watched Monsieur Bardot come with our coffees. When he left I noticed he didn't leave a bill.

"I know you didn't tell me the truth yesterday," I said.

She looked at me but it was impossible to read her eyes.

"Madame Toule wasn't really a man, was she?"

She sighed in the closest thing to an admission I'd ever seen from her. She didn't nod or shake her head or say a single word but she'd answered me nonetheless.

So it was a lie. A lie to throw me off the scent of the real secret.

"Well, I can't imagine a secret that would be worse than that," I said. "The real secret must be a doozy."

Another waiter came to our table and deposited a small carafe of water. Madame C spoke to him and he turned to me.

"Madame Cazaly says the worst secrets always involve other people."

Well, at least I now knew she understood way more than I thought she did.

We sat in silence and drank our coffees. The weather had gotten decidedly cooler. If there had been subtle hints all week that autumn was coming, today erased all doubts. A part of me couldn't believe I was still going to be here for autumn and possibly even winter.

I noticed several people at other tables looking at Madame C and whispering behind their hands. It's true she was a sort of village celebrity—she and her sister both were —but the looks people were giving her had a tinge of something more. Whatever the rumors were about her and the war, these people looked at her with respect but also fear.

She finished her coffee and I knew we would be heading back to *La Fleurette*. Without realizing I meant to do it, I waved down the waiter. Unlike how he responded to my entreaties on most other days, he came immediately.

"Please ask Madame Cazaly how she and Madame Toule were friends," I said, my eyes on Madame C. I knew she understood me. Bringing the waiter over to translate wasn't for her. He was only necessary for me.

Proving my point, Madame C spoke to the waiter and he turned to me.

"She say they were not being friends. But she sad for her."

Felt sorry for her? Pitied her? There has to be more to it than that.

I knew I was close to something. I knew by the way Madame C watched me with her narrowed eyes that she knew I was close to it too.

"One last question," I said to her and she shrugged but her eyes never left mine.

"Why did you choose *her* to pity over so many others? What was special about her?"

The waiter let out an exasperated snort as if taking personal offense at my question but I'd been in France long enough to know to ignore all signs of Gallic peevishness.

Madame C appeared to be thinking about the question. She finally tore her eyes away from me and stared out over the heads of the people in the café enjoying a late afternoon coffee or an early glass of wine. She began to speak and when she did, she looked as though she were going into a trance—or perhaps she was visiting a time gone by.

The waiter cleared his throat and spoke softly.

"Madame C say that Madame Toule is living a life of... loss." The waiter continued to speak as Madame C spoke and I felt my pulse quicken. Madame C's guard was down. If there was ever a time I was going to get the truth, this was it.

"She say to teach so many children but not have one of her own to love....at least not one to keep...is breaking the heart."

I woke up quick.

"What did you mean *not one to keep*? Did Madame Toule lose a child?" I felt the excitement of the revelation filter though me. "Ask her!" I demanded the waiter, going so far as to tug on his sleeve.

But Madame C had snapped out of her reverie—very likely due to the earth-thudding crash landing of my jumping on her last comment like the proverbial duck on a June bug.

Madame C spoke quickly to the waiter who gave a half bow and turned on his heel and left.

"I know you can understand me," I said. "Did Madame Toule have a child? A baby? Did she lose it?"

Madame C pushed her coffee cup away and looked around, preparing to leave and very studiously pretending not to understand me.

I'm pretty sure I would have pushed it—I was so close!—except at that exact moment, one of the women in the café gave a short scream which forced all of us to stand up and see what had happened.

Naturally, because I don't understand French, all I could deduce was that something bad had in fact happened—that was something that everyone by their behavior seemed to be in full agreement on. Everyone in the café was talking all at once and a few even hurried away.

"What in the world has happened?" I said in exasperation and mounting fear. Was it another EMP? Or worse? Were we being invaded?

Madame C reached out and took me by the hand.

Another first.

She squeezed it and began to tug me away from the café.

"*Morte*," she said over her shoulder to me.

Dead? I pulled my hand from her, forcing her to stop and turn to look at me. I didn't need to ask *who* since my face was clearly asking it for me. *Who is dead?*

A couple came over to Madame C and spoke rapidly to her. She nodded in understanding and then looked back at me.

"You come home now," she said. "No help her. Nobody."

I just stared at her because right about then I heard the name of the dead woman being bandied about the outdoor café like a badminton birdie being tossed by the wind.

The dead woman was Juliette Bombre.

19

BUT FOR THE GRACE OF GOD

Luc stared down at Juliette's body.

Like Madame Toule, she was on her back, her eyes open, her throat darkened by terrible bruises and her neck twisted. Unlike Madame Toule, she was nude. Her body found in the bedroom. Her fingernails were broken, a piece of yellow fabric clutched in one hand.

No lab analysis existed any more to help them determine what it was or whose it was.

Eloise knelt by the body. She was wearing gloves but Luc wasn't sure why. They had no way of analyzing the evidence even if they kept it uncontaminated. The medical examiner from Aix had been notified but who knew how long he would take before arriving?

"Who would want to hurt Juliette?" Eloise said softly.

Luc looked up to see Romeo Remey standing in the doorway. As the man glanced down at the body, his old face was mournful and unsurprised.

"A crowd is gathering, Chief," Romeo said.

Luc nodded. "Ask if anybody saw anyone entering Juliette's house. It was broad daylight. Someone should have seen something."

Romeo nodded and left.

Luc looked around Juliette's bedroom. It was neat and feminine. Just as he would have expected from her. This was the first time he'd been in her bedroom. Their only other romantic interaction had started and ended in her living room—the room the killer would have had to walk through to kill Juliette in her bedroom.

"Leave her," Luc said. "See what you can find in the living room."

Eloise nodded and stood and carefully picked her way out of the room.

What did it matter? What did any of it matter? Processing the crime scene—unless there was a weapon visible—was now a useless exercise. For today's crimes they needed eyewitnesses! Or confessions. The evidence had stopped speaking to them...right about the time the EMP had dropped and made forensic science a thing of the past.

Luc picked up a cotton blanket from the bed and draped it over the body.

Who did this to you, chèrie? he thought sadly.

Had she been raped? Or had the killer caught her in a state of undress? The medical examiner would tell them in due time.

Thibault couldn't have done this. Not only was he in police custody but Matteo had driven him to Nice to stand trial two hours earlier.

So this was not a serial killing—not unless Thibault was in fact innocent. In that case, while they'd been wrapping up Thibault's guilt, the real killer had selected his next victim.

Luc thought back to the strawberry cake still sitting on his desk and his stomach buckled.

If only he'd come to see her as he'd planned. If not for a little boy caught in an oak tree, Juliette would still be alive.

By the time Madame C and I walked back to *La Fleurette*—about twenty minutes in which time I'd formally said goodbye to my favorite Dolce Vita flats as anything else now but yard shoes—I'd also tied up the murder case in a neat little bow.

One of the benefits of not speaking a common language is that no matter how many people you're with there's always plenty of time for rumination.

It all seemed so clear to me now! The killer was Romain! It had to be! For one thing, if Juliette really *was* his sister, then Romain was the common denominator in both her and Madame Toule's murders.

The only question I had was motive. I got why he might want to kill the woman who'd seduced him—still nearly impossible to really believe—but why kill his own sister? Plus—and this was only a minor annoyance and because it had to do with fact verification not one that really bothered me too much—there was no proof that Juliette and Romain were related. All I really had was the coincidence of the common name.

As for Madame C's accidental confession that Madame Toule had lost a child, once I got over the excitement of thinking this brand-new piece of info was important, I spent the ensuing twenty minutes trying to make it critical to how Madame Toule died and I just couldn't.

So she had a baby. What did that have to do with how she died?

I was reflecting on exactly that when Madame C and I

reached the front drive of *La Fleurette*. Katrine Pelletier was standing out front with her bike. Madame C went straight into the house and I could see Katrine was in a hurry to get back to the village.

"Hey, what's up?" I said as I reached her.

Katrine looked frazzled. Her fingernails were bitten down where they gripped the bike handles.

She wasted no time with pleasantries.

"Is it true you are going to the special market tonight in Nice?" she asked.

"Where did you hear that?"

"Do you mind if Gaultier goes with you?"

I was surprised. Katrine's jealousy when it came to Gaultier was renowned.

"Sure," I said. "I'd appreciate the company. You're okay with this?"

"I'd prefer he didn't—I've heard the market is dangerous. But when Gaultier heard *les soeurs* were letting you go, there went my argument of how dangerous it was."

"*Letting* me go? They're *making* me go."

I walked with her down our driveway toward the main road to the village.

"How do you know where it's being held?"

"*Les soeurs* know. I get the impression that the location changes constantly so they won't know until just before I leave. I have no idea how they're getting their information."

"Are you bringing any weapons at all?" she asked.

"You mean besides a big strong guy like Gaultier? Nope."

She released a sigh of relief.

"Thanks, Jules. Just please be careful, okay? I've heard terrible things about this market."

"Gosh, Katrine, would *les soeurs* really send me into some place so dangerous? Not to worry!"

"Yeah, right."

"You heard about Juliette?"

"Can you believe it?"

"I'm surprised Gaultier is okay with leaving you home alone with your two little girls with a murderer on the loose."

"Yeah, well. He doesn't love the idea. But I have a rifle and we'll get our month's income with one trip to this market. So who do you think killed Juliette?"

"Well, we know it wasn't Thibault."

"Do you think they'll let him go now?"

"I doubt it. But listen, do you have a minute? I got a little bit of Intel from Madame C just now."

"Is it the big secret?"

"I think so. At least it is as far as she's concerned. It seems that Madame Toule lost a child."

"You mean like a miscarriage?"

I frowned and tried to remember Madame C's exact words. "She didn't say baby—she said *child*."

"Well, I'm positive Madame Toule never had any children."

"That's what makes this such a big secret, don't you see? Madame Toule had a secret child!"

"How is that germane?"

"I don't know! Except, who is he? How old would he be now? When did he die? *How* did he die?"

"*Did* he die?"

"Well, if he didn't die, where is he? And why didn't Madame Toule raise him?"

Katrine raised an eyebrow. "You seem to think we French can just pop out love children with no worries about what a provincial village might think about it. I grant you it is not as bad as a small town in Iowa, possibly, but such a thing still would have been unacceptable—especially in those days."

"Okay," I said, "so, let's say Madame Toule got pregnant—"

"She was always fat. She would easily have been able to hide the fact."

"Exactly. So let's say she had a secret pregnancy. She had the baby, and...and then what?"

"You need to go back and grill the old ladies," Katrine said as she hopped on her bike and began to pedal away. "*They* know what happened to Madame Toule's baby, you can bet your life on that."

20

ONE STEP AT A TIME

As I watched Katrine ride away I knew she was right. But just at the moment I didn't have the energy to wrestle either of the Madame Twins to the ground to get them to tell me any more answers.

It had been exhausting just having coffee with Madame C and finding out as much as I had.

Besides, while I was sure that Madame Toule's mystery baby was somehow connected to her murder—call it intuition—I still didn't know how it all fit in with Juliette's death. I gave myself a moment to feel sorrow for the poor woman who'd died today.

Whether she was Romain's sister or Luc's lover or a sharecropper's daughter, she was a human being who had hopes and dreams—and all of that had been cut short.

I glanced at my watch. It was right at seven in the evening. Even as we were steadily creeping toward fall, there was still enough light in the sky to see without a flashlight and I still had at least an hour before the Madame Twins would be stuffing me in their wine bus and pointing me toward Nice.

I'd already calculated that I'd arrive at the market at eleven in the evening and I felt a sudden rush of gratitude that Katrine's big burly husband would be riding shotgun.

All of which meant I had time to go into town and see Luc again. I hurried back down the road toward the village, mindful that *les soeurs* could come running out at any minute and demand to know why I was leaving. I quickened my pace until I'd rounded the first corner making it impossible for them to see me from the front door.

I imagined Luc would be busy processing this murder since it had just happened and I wasn't completely sure what I hoped to accomplish by seeing him—especially after our last disastrous meeting. But if Juliette really had been special to him then he was hurting in a very specific way right now. And regardless of how we'd left things, or what information or details about the case I might hope to get from him, I really just wanted to see if I could comfort him.

The building the *police municipale* was in was in a blaze of lights by the time I reached it. With a murder like this there would definitely be an all-hands-on-deck mentality and sure enough, as I approached, I saw the station's parttimer, old Romeo Remey standing outside talking with Eloise.

They were both waving away any villagers walking up to ask questions so I guess they'd suspended any and all routine village complaints until they got a handle on this newest murder.

I glanced in the first floor office window—Luc's office—and I could see shadows behind the curtain so I knew he was there. I waited until Eloise saw me and walked over to me as I knew she would.

"How's he doing?" I asked before she could speak.

"Not good. It was a terrible shock."

I knew Eloise was the weak link in Luc's chain of command and I hated that I continued to use her but honestly I really felt I was doing it for all the right reasons.

"How was she killed?" I asked.

Without hesitation (maybe she was just used to responding to orders?) Eloise said, "We think she was raped and then strangled."

Raped? Well, that takes Romain off the hook.

Doesn't it?

"Were there any clues at the crime scene?"

"Nothing we can do anything with. No neighbors heard anything. The guy Juliette was dating is in custody."

Thibault? Juliette was dating Thibault? Of course she was! Juliette was who Thibault was supposed to be meeting in the field! That's who he was trying to protect!

I began to feel a fluttering in my chest, like a trapped bird trying to break free. The pieces were falling into place. Every one of them. The picture was assembling right before my eyes.

"Nothing else?" I asked.

"Nothing helpful. We have a ripped piece of yellow jumper recovered in Juliette's hand. But half the men in Chabanel wear the same workman's jumper. Without the ability to do any kind of laboratory analysis—we'll never find the owner."

I looked in the direction of Luc's office.

"Do you think he'll see me?"

"He feels responsible," Eloise said. "Like he should have protected her."

"Because they were dating?"

Eloise narrowed her eyes at my question. I pretty clearly tipped my hand and hated that she would probably clam up now.

"I don't know about the Chief's personal life," she said.

Of course you don't, I thought. *You and the whole village have no idea who's sleeping with whom, do you?*

I thanked her and went into the police station.

Thank goodness Matteo was nowhere to be seen. He was probably still back at the crime scene or maybe transporting the body to the Aix hospital morgue.

I couldn't reconcile the image of Juliette with her brightly-painted fingernails and her poufy avant-garde hair styles—and the sterile setting of the county morgue.

I went directly to Luc's office and didn't bother knocking. In my experience, knocking—like any other announcement of intention—only gives people an opportunity to deny you.

Luc was sitting at his desk, a typewriter on the desk and a half-drunk bottle of wine before him.

"Hey," I said as I entered.

He looked up with suddenly hopeful eyes as if expecting to see someone else—*Juliette, maybe*?—and his shoulders dropped in disappointment.

I've had better welcomes.

"I wanted to see how you were doing," I said, walking to the desk but deliberately not sitting. He was a lot further gone than I would have guessed. I didn't have time to really talk with him—not and get back to *La Fleurette* in time to avoid the twins' hissy fit I'd never recover from.

"I'm so sorry about Juliette," I said.

Luc's eyes narrowed when I said that and he didn't need to say a word. I saw vividly enough what he was thinking. It was plastered across his face. He thought I was here for information on the case. He thought my asking about him was just a ruse.

Now, granted, I did already get all the information I knew I'd be getting tonight from Eloise. Luc never would have been that forthcoming. And of course I was titanically disappointed that Luc and Juliette had been seeing each other...I guess when she wasn't seeing Thibault? But everything else about my visit was on the level. I fought down my indignation that Luc might see it as self-serving.

"I'm very busy tonight," he said dully. "Eloise should not have allowed you in."

Wow. We really were traversing a whole new set of roads in our relationship tonight. I'd never seen him so cold and distant—not toward me anyway.

Since condolences and attempts at comfort didn't seem to be working, I made what I can only say in hindsight was a critical error in judgment when I decided I'd tell him the facts that I'd uncovered in the case.

Now in my mind this was a way of giving him more ammunition in order to solve not just Madame Toule's murder but also Juliette's! I would have thought he'd be grateful.

But, yeah, no. He so wasn't.

"I wanted to tell you that I found out that Romain Armand—the owner of Bar á GoGo—was the child in the sex scandal with Madame Toule back in 1998," I said.

Luc looked up at me as if I'd begun spouting Swahili.

I knew he was upset so I figured he just needed a little more detail to understand what I was saying.

"And I'm pretty sure nobody's questioned him yet."

Luc just continued to stare at me and now that I know what was on in his mind I cringe that I just kept going. But at the time, I thought he was processing what I was saying like it was a revelation—you know, a key to his investigation —and I couldn't help but think that *this* is why we should be working on this together! He's seeing the bits that had eluded me!

Uh, yeah, no. Not even for a minute.

"Plus," I said, in growing excitement at what I thought was his positive reception at my words, "and I don't know how this fits but it turns out that Romain was probably Juliette's brother. Again, I don't know how that fits—or even if it does..."

Luc stood up, his face red with apoplexy and he shot out an imperious arm to point to the door I'd just come through.

"Get out. And while you're at it, quit maligning a poor woman who isn't dead six whole hours yet!"

"Maligning? How am I maligning her?"

Although it's true if you were to take my theory to it's logical conclusion—which thank God it looked like I was not going to get the chance to do—it had Juliette at the center of it.

Possibly as the murderer with her brother Romain as her stooge.

I'm so glad I hadn't yet put that theory into so many words in my mind. And even gladder that I hadn't put it into words with Luc.

"I cannot believe you would come here to disparage Juliette on the very day she has been brutally murdered!"

I swear I felt my blood pressure rocket to the top of my head, I was so frustrated with him!

"And I can't believe you're acting like a bereaved husband," I said hotly, "instead of the professional investigator you're supposed to be!" I have to say I was frankly astonished at the words that had just come out of my mouth.

Luc must have been too because he just stared at me.

But I wasn't done yet. Heaven help us all.

"Stop making this about *you* and however guilty *you* feel about not being who Juliette hoped you'd be with her," I said. "Pull yourself together! There's still a murderer running around and now he's an effing serial killer! Who *else* gets to die before you stop focusing on Thibault and start questioning the right people?"

As with most things I do, I went too far. I mean waaaaaay too far. That was evident by the horror-struck expression on Luc's face.

You know how you sometimes see a thing change forever right before your eyes? Like maybe the last wrench on a water pipe just before it breaks and explodes noxious sewer water everywhere?

Yeah. Luc's face. Like that.

All I knew was that more words out of my mouth would, if not make it worse, certainly not fix or unsay the terrible things I'd already said.

Not trusting myself to say anything less horrible, I staggered backward and fled out of the police building feeling ashamed and hating myself.

I didn't even look at Eloise as I hurried past her.

In the end it had been relatively easy to find the location of tonight's market, Romain thought as he left the alley where his contact had met him. His wine co-op contact Jacques had been initially surprised that Romain was interested— after all, what did he have to sell? Or buy for that matter?

Romain walked quickly down the narrow alley, the refuse of last night's street wash running between his feet.

But there were other uses for a venue where death holds court, Romain thought.

This morning Jean-Michel the man who sold Romain his olives for the bar had mentioned in the way of gossip that *les soeurs* were planning on going to the special Nice market tonight to sell their homemade wine.

Of course it was not the old women themselves who would be going, Jean-Michel had said, but the American living with them.

That was the moment when Romain knew the market was his answer—his only answer. There was no possibility of taking the American anywhere in Chabanel. She was too closely watched by the chief of police, not to mention *les soeurs.*

But to be alone at night at the market known for its "accidental deaths?"

It was as if it was preordained. Written in the stars.

Meant to be.

How she came to know his secret, he did not know. Before he slit her throat he would get the answer to that so that his secret—his and Juliette's secret—might go back into the vault, safe and shielded once more.

And even if his latest information about that idiot Pelletier driving to the market with the American tonight was correct, it didn't matter. He remembered Gaultier from school. The moron was bigger now but he was still afraid of his own shadow. He would be no problem. He'd have to kill him too, of course, and Romain felt a surge of determination at the thought.

None of them had stood by him all those years ago. Not a one. Not a single friend had defended him or supported him. When he thought of that terrible year before his family moved away, he felt the humiliation as vividly as if it had just happened.

The shame of knowing the whole village believed he had slept with his fat schoolteacher, Madame Toule was unbearable.

They all thought it. Even his friends. His so-called friends.

Romain shook his head as he walked faster, his muscles quivering.

No, having Gaultier along would not be a problem at all.

It would be a bonus.

21

COMING TOGETHER

I'm trying to remember if there was another time in my life when I felt worse. I kept hearing my words to Luc coming back at me. Most particularly: *Who else gets to die before you start questioning the right people?*

What in the world made me say that? Well, okay, I know what made me say it. I was frustrated. And I was hurt, if I'm honest. I was hurt at how bereft Luc appeared over Juliette's death. It was clear he must have really loved her.

I'd accused him of making her death all about him but now I was doing the very same thing only for different reasons.

Juliette's death was not about Luc or me. It was its own tragedy and needed to be mourned for exactly that. With a deep breath, I officially refused to allow myself to feel sorry for myself when it came to Luc loving Juliette—at least until the poor woman had been dead and buried at least a year.

Satisfied with this very mature plan of self-flagellation, I focused on helping *les soeurs* pack up the last crates of their blackberry wine into Thibault's car.

Again, because we don't speak the same language, being

with the twins was always an exercise in being alone. I listened to them talk back and forth to each other—still hoping to understand some of it through osmosis—and found my thoughts straying back to the case.

Madame Toule, dead by strangulation.

Juliette, dead two days later. By strangulation.

Where was the intersecting point between these two?

I figured Juliette had to be at least twelve years younger than Romain. That meant she was born around the time of the scandal. A cold thought drifted into my bones and made me shiver.

What if it was true that Pauline had slept with the young Romain? *What if she'd gotten pregnant by him? And what if that baby was Juliette?*

Ignoring for the moment the logistics of how Madame Toule's baby got stuck in Romain's family to be raised that would make Juliette Romain's *daughter*, not his sister.

But why would Pauline give the baby to Romain's parents to raise? Well, if they were the grandparents, it might make some sense. Was she afraid of reprisals from the village? Visions of tar and feathers came to mind.

I struggled to picture Pauline Toule, pregnant or newly delivered of her baby.

I loaded the last wine crate into the back seat of the car —the trunk now completely full. There was a chill in the air and I noticed that one of the Madame Twins had brought me a jacket and placed a hamper of food on the floor of the car. I pulled on the jacket and took in a deep breath.

At eight o'clock, the light was nearly gone from the sky and I was breathing in the last of the summer yellow broom flowers as well as the honeysuckle. I wondered what Luc was doing right now.

What if I came at this from a different angle? What if

Madame Toule had an affair with the *father*—Gerard Toulouse? Maybe he promised to leave his family for her or something. Then leaving the baby on the Toulouse family doorstep suddenly made much more sense.

I felt a tingle of excitement at this new approach. So much so that it took me a moment to realize the twins were reacting to a shadow approaching us from the drive.

"*Bonsoir, La Fleurette!*" Jim Anderson sang out, in order to let us know it was only him.

I greeted him with the usual cheek kissing ritual.

"I thought I'd drop by to let you know there's a major town hall meeting in the morning and everyone is supposed to attend," Jim said.

"Because of the murders?" I said.

"Presumably." He turned to the twins and told them in French about the morning's meeting. Watching him talk with *les soeurs* gave me an idea.

"Jim, would you ask the twins a question for me?"

"Sure."

"Ask them if Juliette Bombre was Pauline Toule's daughter?"

"Jules," Jim said admonishingly. "Give the poor woman a break."

"I'm not maligning her! I'm trying to find out who killed her! Ask them."

Jim sighed and turned to the twins and spoke to them. When he finished, they exchanged a look and Madame C shrugged and nodded.

Jim was astonished. "*Vraiment?*" he said.

"Okay," I said. "Now ask them if Juliette was the product of Pauline's relationship with Romain Toulouse—now Romain Armand."

Jim hesitated just a second and then translated my question.

Madame C snorted and said a few words with an eye roll.

"She said *don't be ridiculous*," Jim translated.

"Then who?" I asked Madame C directly.

"*Je ne sais pas*," she said.

"I know you *do* know," I said heatedly. "And it matters. Now more than ever because if the baby was Romain's, he's a suspect in Juliette's murder but it if the baby was his father's—"

"What difference does that make?" Jim asked, running a hand through his head as he tried to process what he was hearing.

"It makes a difference because someone killed Madame Toule and her daughter too! Ask them if Juliette was born *before* Romain's family moved away? Or after?"

"*Après*," Madame Becque said. *After.*

Juliette was Madame Toule's illegitimate baby. That meant her killer had to be Romain! All the evidence pointed to him. He was physically capable of doing it. He had no alibi and he had motive.

I paused at that. What *was* his motive? Being made a fool of at thirteen? Being forced to be raised either with his own child or that of his father's mistress? Something was missing here.

But if Madame Toule's killer wasn't Romain, then who was it? And then my other theory came back to me. The one I was hesitant to even think about because of that whole *don't think ill of the dead* thing. The one that I could not even breathe the possibility of—at least not to Jim or Luc both of whom felt I wasn't objective when it came to Juliette.

Juliette was to meet Thibault in the meadow because

she needed him *not* to have an alibi. And a good reason why she might need him not to have an alibi was because she was planning on pinning Madame Toule's murder on him. A murder she wouldn't commit herself because of physical limitations, but one planned and driven by her all the same.

A sudden image of the blue flecks of paint on the rug in Madame Toule's house came to me. Paint that perfectly matched Juliette's manicure. Paint that might easily come off if one were lobbing a chunk of rock through a window.

I felt a tingle of excitement jolt through me as another thought hit me.

What if Juliette and Romain had a *special* brother and sister bond? The kind that was taboo in any society—even France? What if Juliette—who had motive out the ying yang for wanting her mother dead—convinced her brother to kill her mother, then steal the mug so Juliette could plant it in Thibault's apartment?

The true murderer might be dead, I thought grimly, but her murder weapon—Romain Armand—was very much alive.

"Where are you going with all this?" Jim said, breaking me out of my reverie.

For a minute I thought he was reading my mind but then I noticed he was looking at the loaded car of wine.

The Madame Twins had made a big deal about me not telling anyone about my trip to Nice tonight. *Boy, those two make keeping secrets a living art.* But I'd promised not to tell anyone.

"It's for tomorrow's market in Aix," I said.

"I thought it was impossible to park in Aix without getting your car stolen."

"I don't intend to be there that long."

Jim frowned and then shrugged. And as he said his

goodbyes and headed back down the road toward Chabanel, I was in a fog of swirling thoughts and revelations.

You know how when you finally stumble across the truth of a thing you can't believe you hadn't seen it before because it was so obvious?

Like that.

Juliette and Romain had conspired together to kill Madame Toule. It was Juliette's revenge against the mother who'd either slept with her brother or supposed grandfather and then had given the baby up—given Juliette up—no doubt to be tortured by her stepmother—a woman who by all accounts was cold and spiteful. Then, for whatever reason—a lover's quarrel?—the two of them fell out and Juliette ended up dead.

There was no doubt in my mind. Romain was our double murderer.

I felt a sudden flash of urgency. *I had to get to Luc and tell him.* Once I showed him all the steps leading up to it, I just knew he'd see it too!

Madame C frowned and tapped her wristwatch and jerked her head in the direction of the fully loaded car.

And I would do exactly that. Just as soon as I got back from Nice.

22

THE FULL MONTY

L uc sat in his desk chair and stared at the basket which he knew held the strawberry cake. He hadn't even had the chance to tell Juliette thank you. She'd clearly made it by hand. That was something people didn't know about her. Everyone thought she was shallow, even cheap. But she was a baker at heart.

She loved to bake.

He tore his eyes away from the basket and stared out the window in the direction of *La Fleurette*.

He couldn't stop himself from shaking his head at the thought of Jules. At the thought of the words she'd flung at him not an hour earlier.

And at the realization that she'd been so right about all of it.

How could he have taken his guilt and failure out on her like that? Hadn't he used his own sense of loss as an excuse? Since when did he allow himself excuses?

He would stop by *La Fleurette* later tonight—as usual— to apologize to her. It wasn't her fault that he used Juliette and then couldn't protect her. It was only her fault that she was able to see it and put it into words. And for that, perversely, he thought he might actually love her.

Eloise stepped into the office. "Did you call me, Chief?"

He glanced at her. She was mid twenties. Too young to remember the scandal with Madame Toule in 1998.

"No. But let me ask you. Had you heard about the sex scandal with Madame Toule and a student twenty-two years ago?"

She shrugged. "Everyone's heard of it."

"Did you ever know anyone personally connected with it? A classmate of the boy, perhaps?"

An older brother, maybe? A cousin?

She shook her head.

Luc looked back at the strawberry cake basket. Was Jules right? Was Romain the boy in the scandal? If so why did he return? Why did he change his name? Was Juliette really his sister?

"Has anyone questioned Romain Armand in the Madame Toule murder?" Luc asked. But he knew the answer.

"Why would they?"

Why indeed.

If Romain really was Juliette's brother, he would be a good person to talk to.

"Chief?" Eloise said. "The Medical Examiner is finished with the body."

Luc stood up. He knew he'd get the report in the morning or, more likely, tomorrow evening, now that it had to be typed up and driven back to Chabanel. Gone were the days of faxes and email attachments.

"I'll talk to him before he goes," he said, grabbing his jacket off his chair. "And do me favor, Eloise." He gestured to the cake basket on the edge of his desk. "Take that away. I think it's starting to mold."

I could see how worried Katrine was about packing up her precious Gaultier for the Nice market. Honestly, the dude was as big as a double wide but it was cute to see how protective she was of him.

The two of them arrived minutes before it was time to leave. They'd brought their inventory of cheeses on a bike cart. Katrine was the one pedaling the cart. I would've thought that was the man's job but I guess there was the argument that Gaultier walking ahead with the flashlight to light the way made more sense since he could easily stay ahead of the wagon with his long strides.

Even so, Katrine arrived at *La Fleurette* panting and red in the face. In all fairness, Gaultier made her sit down while he transferred the packages of cheese from the cart to the car.

By this time it was downright cold—the first real cold snap that I'd felt since being in the south of France. We were all wearing thick jackets. The Madame Twins supervised the loading of the cheese like they were army loadmasters. All they lacked were clipboards and police whistles.

I overheard them speaking sternly to Gaultier and while I didn't understand what they said to him I'm pretty sure it involved the demand for a percentage of his profits for providing the lift to Nice.

Wow. Those two were ruthless. But hey, they liked their cheese and were probably not going to pass up an obvious opportunity to make a tidy sum in goat cheese when it was in the offing.

Since I couldn't do anything at present with the information that I'd learned about Madame Toule—or my new theory about who killed her—I put thoughts of both the murders out of my mind at least until I returned from Nice later tonight or—more likely—really early tomorrow morning.

Gaultier had asked to drive which suited me fine and as he and Katrine indulged in a very mushy moment of saying goodbye reminiscent of what it must been like when soldiers went off to war, Madame B took me aside and handed me an object wrapped in an old towel.

Thinking it was more food for the trip, I was about to make a joke when I felt the hard angles of the gun in my hands. I peeled back one flap of the towel to see a World War II German Luger.

"You will be...*faites attention*," she said. I think she meant *be safe* so I just nodded with that assumption.

"It's loaded, I suppose," I said, breathlessly, hefting the weapon in my hands. I'd never fired a gun before. I'm not embarrassed to say I was basically afraid of them, like I expected them to jump up and shoot me with no help from anyone else.

Did Madame B really think I'd be capable of firing this at someone? Or was it just for show? Because if that was the case I wasn't too keen about waving around a loaded pistol.

She smiled and nodded, having not understand what I said but answered me just the same.

I looked at Gaultier over her head and he smiled.

"Just put it in the glovebox," he said. "We won't need it. I am sure of that."

Yeah, right. So much for *this market is not at all dangerous.* It's as safe as zipping down to your local Whole Foods.

In Kabul.

I stashed the gun in the glove box and said goodbye to the Madame Twins. Katrine was standing next to Gaultier as if afraid to let him out of her sight. For someone who did so much complaining about how oppressed she felt in her marriage, she was doing a pretty good impersonation of the clingy wife.

She didn't get eye contact with me which seriously annoyed me but which I chalked up to her jealousy over Gaultier. I thought we'd gotten past all that but I suppose once a pathology, always a pathology.

I got in the car and could tell that it would ride much lower than it had when I drove it to *La Fleurette*. It was literally packed to the gunnels.

"Let's go, Gaultier," I called. "The sooner we're there the sooner we're on the way back."

"*D'accord*," he said, giving Katrine a last kiss before sliding into the driver's seat. I heard him murmur to her, "*Nous allons bien, chérie. Ne pas s'inquiéter.*"

After Luc had spoken to the medical examiner and seen the verbal report on the findings—rape and death by asphyxiation—he sat outside the station and smoked a cigarette. It shouldn't have been a surprise.

It wasn't a surprise.

Before Eloise left for the day, she'd also handed in her preliminary report compiled from Romeo's canvassing of Juliette's street.

Nobody had seen anything. They saw no one enter her house. They saw no one leave.

Two murders within three days of each other. Both strangulations. It had to be the same person. It was impossible to believe Chabanel had two murderers operating in the same week. And if it was the same man, of course it was not Thibault Theroux, who was safely tucked away in the arms of the Nice *Police Municipale* by now.

What leads did they have? Who else did they talk to? He rubbed a hand across his face. In the morning, he would send Eloise to the Chabanel market to see who had spoken with Juliette there yesterday. He would find out the gossip if there was any to hear. Who did Juliette flirt with? Who knew her? Who had suspicions about something that might have been going on with her?

He tossed his cigarette in the street and watched the smoke curl into the night until it finally died away. Then he stood and walked across the street.

It wasn't really a lead, of course, but it was better than sitting on a stone bench at nine at night wondering why they hadn't questioned a single other soul except Thibault Theroux regarding the Madame Toule murder.

Luc knew Bar á GoGo would be open of course and its proprietor would no doubt be manning the bar. Luc didn't know Romain Armand well but well enough over the years. He tried to remember if he'd ever had a personal conversation with Armand beyond the basic civilities.

The fact was he didn't really know anything at all about Romain Armand. If he was in fact Juliette's brother, that was excuse enough why Luc might want to have a word. If nothing else, to offer his condolences. And if Romain denied the relationship, well that would be interesting too.

The bar was two streets over tucked between a butcher shop and a store that used to be a dress shop but was now permanently closed. The night air had turned cold and the tables and chairs normally out on the terrace were gone.

People would have to take their drinks inside the bar tonight, Luc thought, as he entered.

Even before the EMP had happened, this bar had been dark inside. Now lanterns were strategically set around the room allowing just enough light for people to find their drinks. It wasn't full by any means, Luc thought, but Romain would do a decent business tonight. He scanned the room and then glanced at the bar.

The young man Romain had hired was wiping down the bar. Luc approached.

"Where is your boss tonight?" Luc said.

A loud thump came from overhead and both the young man and Luc looked upward. Romain lived over the bar.

"Never mind," Luc said. "I think I found him."

Going out the back door of the bar, Luc stepped into a dank, narrow alley. To his immediate left was a wooden staircase leading up to Romain's apartment. Directly in front of him was a parked and chained scooter.

Luc frowned. He didn't remember anyone in Chabanel having a scooter. It was part of his business to know these things.

Perhaps it was new.

Another thudding sound came from the top of the stairs that sounded like the sound of a door slamming shut. Luc stepped into the shadows and waited. It occurred to him to call out to Romain, surely something anyone might do if they were looking to talk to someone. So he couldn't account for the fact that he decided not to do that.

Chalk it up to a policeman's instinct.

A part of him knew he needed to take Romain by surprise.

Romain came down the stairs. He was a tall man, but not bulky. In his role as publican, he was usually smiling and talkative but tonight his face was frozen into a mask of humorless determination.

As Romain hit the final step, Luc turned on his flashlight and illuminated the man from head to toe.

Immediately, he saw the large knife scabbard hanging on Romain's belt and the hand gun jammed into the waistband.

"Going somewhere, Romain?" Luc said, keeping his voice calm and already regretting leaving his own gun on his desk back at the station.

Romain looked at him in stark astonishment that quickly morphed into a cold glare.

Luc could see the next steps play out in his mind seconds before they happened. He saw the decision on Romain's face when he reached it and he saw the second that decision translated into action.

Romain pulled the gun, pointed it at Luc and fired.

23

DEAD TO RIGHTS

One thing you have to say about the apocalypse: there is very little traffic.

Gaultier and I got on the A8 within minutes of leaving *La Fleurette*. I could tell Gaultier was in a good mood. Most men are when they're behind the wheel of a strange car especially when they haven't been able to drive in four months.

The heater in the car was working and both Gaultier and I peeled off our jackets within a few miles and relaxed for a comfortable drive headed east to Nice. I'd never been to Nice—and honestly I wasn't really going to see it this trip either since we were heading to the road around it and not the coast it was famous for.

The first thing Gaultier did when we hit the road was try the radio and we both laughed ruefully at his hope. There might be a radio station somewhere in France—or Europe —but it would be years before we'd be able to dial one in.

With the lack of traffic and the straight shot on the highway toward Nice, I allowed myself a few moments to try to phrase my argument for the case to Luc when I got back.

After all, the last time I'd seen him I'd left him pretty angry. I would have to have an ironclad case with facts that made it so even he could see where they pointed.

I knew if I were smart I wouldn't mention how or why I felt Juliette was involved in Madame Toule's death. Professional investigator or not, Luc was too sensitive about that. My best ploy was to lay out all the facts and hope he came to it on his own. That way also had the added bonus that he wouldn't forever hate me for uncovering the fact that his lady love was a ruthless murderer.

Win win.

To me, it was now so obvious how it all shook out. Juliette had framed poor Thibault to deflect guilt away from her brother who killed her biological mother for her.

Once Luc arrested Romain and got him into the interrogation room he could find out whatever Romain's reason had been for then killing Juliette, his half sister.

Or possibly his daughter.

In any case, probably the reason would have something to do with Romain's very bad temper.

"You are warm enough?" Gaultier asked as he fiddled with the heater knob.

"Yeah, I'm good. Boy, Katrine was really nervous about our taking this trip, wasn't she?"

He laughed. "My wife is a passionate woman."

Was he really such a lunkhead that he didn't know how unhappy Katrine was?

"She's been kind of blue," I said. "Lately."

He glanced at me as if unsure how much to reveal or how much I knew but he nodded his head.

"*Oui*," he said. "*Je sais.*" I know.

"It's hard trying to do all that Katrine does," I said. "Make a living and raise two little girls."

"She is a wonderful mother."

I hadn't met their two little girls yet but I had every expectation that they were darling and well-behaved. Pretty hard not to be with a mother like Katrine who obviously adored them and would work her fingers to the bone and put herself in an early grave to give them what they needed.

In for a penny...

"I think she thinks you could do more with the kids," I said. This was either going to lose me a friend, make the next three hours of driving completely unbearable, or help Katrine in her unhappiness.

"You think my wife and I don't talk about what she needs?"

He didn't say it in an ugly way. But very matter of fact.

"Sorry if I offended. I just know a lot of married couples who don't communicate very well."

That was a lie. I officially knew no married couples at all unless you counted Katrine and Gaultier.

"No offense taken," he said. "You are her friend." He turned to look at me—after all with no cars anywhere in sight there was hardly any reason to watch the road. "You are a good friend to her."

"I hope so."

We drove in silence for awhile. I figured if he already knew he should help more with the kids and Katrine was still unhappy then either he *wasn't* helping out even after knowing he should or there was something else going on.

I decided to change the subject.

"Pretty horrible about Juliette Bombre," I said. "Did you know her?"

"She sold her nuts two stands away from our cheese stand."

I found myself wondering why Katrine hadn't been

jealous of Juliette? Juliette was definite vamp material and she sashayed herself daily in front of Gaultier at the market. Was there a reason Katrine didn't feel threatened by her? Or had I just not picked up on it?

"She was beautiful," I said. "It's always painful when someone that beautiful dies so young."

"Yes, it is true."

Had Gaultier had a fling with Juliette? There has to be a reason why Katrine is psycho jealous around him all the time. Had he stepped out of bounds earlier in their marriage? I figured a tiny bit of pushing would help me find out a little bit more about Katrine and why she was so untrusting of her husband.

"Did you know Juliette was dating the police chief, Luc Debray?" I asked innocently.

He frowned. "I have not heard that."

"Well, she was a woman of mystery, that's for sure. And she had a secret. Did you know that?"

"All women have secrets," he said. He paused and then said, "Juliette's secrets were always going to get her killed."

Whoa! I don't know what Gaultier knew but he clearly knew more than I did.

The question now was *how* did he know?

"Are you talking about the fact that Juliette was Pauline Toule's love child?" I said.

He looked at me in surprise. At first I thought he was reacting to the news that Juliette was Madame Toule's illegitimate child but something about the way he looked at me made me realize he already knew that.

He didn't think anybody *else* knew about it.

How could Gaultier know this about Juliette?

The exhausting process of prying it out of *les soeurs* had given me every reason to believe that *nobody* else in the village knew Madame Toule's secret. So how had Gaultier found out? Was Katrine's jealousy about him justified? *Had* he done more than flirt with Juliette?

Because this secret was not the sort of thing one revealed during an innocent flirtation in broad day light at the city market over cheese and cashews.

This secret was the sort of thing divulged during pillow talk.

Suddenly, the one thing that had bothered me about the whole Juliette-Romain theory came sidling up beside me: To make my theory work I had to have the two involved in an incestuous relationship.

But what if it wasn't incest?

What if everything else was the same—Juliette framed Thibault and used her lover to kill her biological mother—except she didn't use her brother—to do it?

The only things I knew about Romain that I thought made him a good candidate for a murderer was that he had a bad temper and he was connected to both victims.

But what if Juliette's partner was someone else? Someone she didn't have to commit incest with in order to get him to do her bidding?

My stomach lurched as my mind whirled with this new idea that took Romain off the hook and set up...who?

"Did you pack a basket? I know *les soeurs* are famous for their *gougères*."

"It's in the back," I said, my body telling me something that my mind was too slow to realize.

I was afraid. I was suddenly sickeningly afraid.

"Can you get it?" Gaultier asked. "If there is fruit, we don't need to stop. You can feed grapes to me like Cleopatra to Marc Anthony."

"I'm not sure how Katrine would like that," I said, hearing my voice shake.

Quit imagining things! So Gaultier knew Juliette! That doesn't mean he was sleeping with her! And even if he was sleeping with her, that doesn't mean he killed her!

"My wife is very tolerant, no? Even if I get very fat, she will always love me!"

I pulled the hamper out of the back onto my lap. The Madame Twins had packed as if they expected me to be gone a week. I pulled out a bacon and pepper sandwich and peeled back the paper and handed it to Gaultier.

Why was I afraid? What was my body reacting to? This was *Gaultier*! Katrine's clueless big lug of a husband, not a serial killer!

I took in a long breath and let it out and felt instantly better.

"*Merde!*" Gaultier said pawing at his chest. "The mustard is spilling on my shirt."

"Hold on," I said. "They packed *serviettes*."

I dug out two paper napkins and turned to Gaultier and directed my flashlight beam onto his chest where the blob of mustard was.

Right next to the ripped hole on his left breast pocket of his yellow jumper.

24

HELL TO PAY

L uc felt the bullet slice into his arm as he dove behind the trash cans in the alley. That split second of warning when he guessed what Romain was going to do had saved his life.

Knowing he wasn't safe for long among the trash cans—or that the sound of the gunshot would bring help in time—Luc leapt to his feet and flung one of the refuse can lids into Romain's face. The man was half turned toward his bike when Luc hit him.

Romain staggered, his gun limp in his hand as Luc, fueled by fury and pain, tackled him to the ground. He wrenched the gun from Romain's hand and jerked both the man's arms behind his back. With Luc's now badly bleeding arm protesting loudly, he handcuffed Romain, then sat back panting.

"Romain Armand," Luc said, "you are under arrest for assaulting an officer." How badly he wanted to add *and for the suspicion of murder* but it was enough that he had him. The rest would come.

. . .

Two hours later, Luc sat in his office with Eloise. Fortunately the medical examiner had stayed in Chabanel for dinner and was able to clean and treat Luc's wound—a deep graze but not serious.

Romain sat in the single Chabanel jail cell. When he'd stopped weeping, he'd blurted out tearful answers to every question Luc had asked him—as though he'd been waiting for someone to ask him for twenty-two years—as well as a constant stream of apologies for shooting him.

Luc was exhausted, the adrenalin that had driven him for the earlier part of the evening was long gone now. He looked at Eloise. "I thought I told you to go home at the normal time tonight."

"I thought that meant only if someone didn't come pounding on my door with reports of shots fired," she said.

Luc raised an eyebrow but he was glad to finally see some defiance in her. Not too much, but a little fire on the job would serve her well.

"Why did you go to talk to him without your weapon?" Eloise asked.

Luc shook his head. That was stupid. But it was because he hadn't really considered Romain a threat or even a suspect in any way. He was merely attempting to quiet the soft voice in his head—*Jules' voice*—that said he needed to check Armand out.

"I can't believe you solved the case. Just like that!" Eloise said.

Just like that.

"It's not finished until we get a confession," Luc reminded her.

But they'd get it. Luc knew they would. And Jules had been right all along.

Romain was Juliette's brother and the murderer of both Juliette and Madame Toule.

Romain had tearfully divulged that in a desperate bid to garner more attention from his cold and brittle mother, Romain had told his parents that Madame Toule had inappropriately touched him. He'd gotten the idea when he'd seen Madame Toule and his father in a passionate embrace one afternoon in the empty halls of the school.

While telling the world—but mostly his mother—that he'd been sexually molested by Madame Toule had initially had the desired effect of garnering him more attention, in the end the plan had backfired spectacularly.

Not only had his friends been forbidden to play with him, but his family felt forced to leave Chabanel. Worst of all, they'd been saddled with Madame Toule and his father's love child—a child who by her very existence provoked Romain's mother to daily heights of rage and abuse on both children.

While Romain had yet to confess to killing Madame Toule or his sister, Luc had no doubt the confession was forthcoming.

"We should be celebrating," Eloise said as she poured herself a glass of wine from the bottle on Luc's desk.

"A young woman died today," Luc said.

"Her death wasn't your fault."

"Maybe not. But I feel responsible all the same. I led her to believe something that wasn't true."

This is the wine talking and probably a very good reason why policemen should not drink.

"You want the American."

He looked at Eloise in surprise. "Is it that obvious?"

"Only to every woman in Chabanel."

"Do you think Juliette knew?"

"Probably. But if it's any consolation, the American doesn't seem to."

He groaned and put his head in his hands.

"Go home, Chief. Sleep it off. Armand will still be ready to confess in the morning. And everything will look better then."

Luc almost felt like laughing.

In a country known for its love of philosophy, it might not sound like much but in the end Eloise's words were right on the mark. He knew he *must* be drunk because he felt the wisdom in them—tomorrow would be better.

He put his head down on the desk and within moments was fast asleep.

25

DOUBLE WHAMMY

*G*aultier was Juliette's killer.

As I watched Gaultier wipe the mustard stain from his work overalls, my mind flashed in a million different directions—not the least of which was how to get out of the car without getting myself killed.

Gaultier nonchalantly took another bite from the sandwich and I realized that he didn't know I was onto him.

He killed Juliette. Could there be another explanation for the torn uniform? And the fact that he knew her secret?

And if he killed Juliette, then it meant he probably killed Madame Toule too.

My stomach was churning as we thundered down the road, the warmth in the car now suffocating me.

I had to get out. I had to get away from him.

Without knowing what I was doing, my hand slowly moved toward the glove box.

"If you are going for the gun," Gaultier said calmly, "I can break your wrist before you undo the latch. Reconsider."

The terror began to crawl up my throat at his words.

He knows that I know.

"There is no more food?" He glanced at me and then down at the hamper on my lap. "Another sandwich perhaps? No?"

Dear God, Katrine is married to a serial killer. Our cheese vendor at the village market is an effing serial killer.

"Why did you do it?" I said in a small, helpless voice.

We were barely thirty minutes out of Chabanel with at least another three hours to Nice. Even if I did manage to get out of the car, where would I go? And how? On foot?

"Why did I do what? Kill Madame Toule?" He shrugged. "That was a favor for a friend. Madame Toule was my teacher, you know." He shook his head and smiled. "I thought she liked me best. A pet, you know what I'm saying?"

I stared at him in horror. I was getting his confession. Oh, Lord, I was getting his confession like it was the last thing I was ever going to hear in my life.

"But in the end, she did not know me from any of the others. You know?"

"A favor," I said, forcing my voice to stay calm. "You did a favor for Juliette. She asked you to kill Madame Toule for her."

"*C'est vrai*," he said, his eyes on the quiet empty road before us as if picturing Juliette in his mind.

"Did she tell you why?"

Was I stalling? Was there any point to that?

Well, yes, if the point is die now or die later, I choose later.

"Madame Toule gave her up to live with a woman who detested her."

"And Romain had nothing to do with any of it?"

He frowned. "Romain? He went away many, many years ago."

Gaultier didn't know that Romain had returned and was

living under a different name. Or that he was Juliette's brother.

So much for Juliette sharing all her secrets.

"If you killed Madame Toule, why did she scream out Thibault's name?"

He grinned. "I identified myself as Thibault. It had been over twenty years. She never could tell any of us boys a part."

"Was that so the cops would arrest Thibault? How did you know he didn't have an alibi?"

"Because I knew he was out in the middle of a field waiting for Juliette to show up."

So I was right about that. Now if I'd only sorted it all out a little bit sooner I might not be trapped in a car on a deserted road with a double murderer.

"And then you took the coffee mug from Madame Toule's house and gave it to Juliette to plant in Thibault's apartment," I said.

"Very smooth, yes?"

"Why did you kill Juliette?"

"She would not give me what she promised. She thought she was in love with someone else."

I didn't have time to feel sorry for poor unloved, murderous Juliette. I turned to see the darkened landscape rush by and tried to focus my thoughts.

"What now?" I said and instantly regretted it. *Did I really want to know?*

"I am told the Nice market is very dangerous," he said, not smiling now, his eyes on the road ahead. "No one will be surprised if you do not return to Chabanel."

"So you intend to kill me as you did Juliette and Madame Toule." I couldn't believe I was saying the words. Maybe a part of me was trying to rob them of their power or even reconcile myself to the fact that I was going to die. I certainly didn't worry about giving him any ideas he didn't already have.

Which is why he surprised me.

"I fear you will *wish* I had killed you, *chérie*," he said as he glanced over at my chest.

He intends to sell me at the market!

A more sane person would have realized that not being strangled immediately was a good thing and if he intended to put me up for the highest bidder in Nice it meant I had more time—the whole car ride and possibly a chance to escape once we stopped.

But yeah, me and sanity...not so much.

I don't know why I chose then over any other time except to say there wasn't a whole lot of planning or thinking going on. Like the hand with the mind of its own inching toward the glove box, I just moved without knowing I was going to.

I heaved the hamper into his lap and wrenched open my door. I felt his hand grab my hair as I was half way out but I didn't care.

Staying in that car was not an option.

I felt the fire in my scalp as he yanked on me as I tried futilely to launch myself out of the moving car. The pain was unbearable but the alternative was unthinkable.

The car swerved violently and in a fusillade of French curse words, I felt him release me.

I was out the door, the rushing ground along the verge of the road jumped up to slam into my face like a flying cement truck.

26

HELL IN A HAND BASKET

In the end I didn't roll so much as succumb to the laws of nature as my propulsion hurled me down a steep grassy ditch that lined the A8. My ears were full of a roaring sound that blotted out all else. I think the roar was my own terror screaming inside my head. When I finally stopped rolling, I instantly scrambled to my feet—astonished that I felt nothing broken. We must not have been going as fast as I thought we were.

On top of the incessant roaring in my head was the sound of a man screaming. In a miracle I will never believe I deserved, I still had my flashlight in my hand. I wasn't stupid enough to turn it on but having it gave me comfort.

I ran down the ditch, feeling now the abrasion on my hip where I'd hit the ground, and praying the ditch was clear of obstacles that I wouldn't have been able to see until I was falling over them.

I still couldn't hear over the roaring in my ears to tell if Gaultier was running after me. Would he do that? Would he leave the car?

The sound of a gunshot exploding in the night air told

me he would.

I dove to the ground, expecting any minute to feel fire erupt in some part of my body that would tell me I'd been hit. I crawled to the west side of the ditch, with my back to the road and tried desperately to think!

If he had a flashlight, he'd find me sooner or later. I wouldn't be able to outrun him. But if I just waited here, he'd find me as soon as it was daylight.

Surely to God he didn't have that kind of discipline and patience?

I didn't think *I* did and *I* was fighting for my life.

I tried to hear if he was coming after me but the roaring in my ears made it impossible to detect anything but the voice in my head that screamed *Run!*

If Gaultier was smart he'd go through the basket the sisters had packed to see if there was another flashlight there.

Knowing them, there would be.

Once he found it, he'd jump into the ditch and come after me.

I had to get moving. Anything was better than being found cowering in this ditch waiting for him to come and blow my brains out.

Gaultier was borderline fat. He might not have the stamina to go as long as I was sure I could—driven by terror and the desire to stay alive.

At this point, it was all I had. I eased myself out of my corner of the ditch and began to run.

Katrine saw the tail lights of the car up ahead and her heart sank. Yes, she'd been hoping to catch up before it was too late, but seeing the car parked and idling in the middle of the road—not even pulled off onto the shoulder—told her that her worst fears were being realized.

Gaultier and Jules were in that car, laughing at everyone who'd never suspected that they were lovers. Jules was enjoying the same caresses that Katrine had always felt were her province alone. Gaultier was looking at Jules the way he looked at Katrine. The image was so powerful and so nauseating that Katrine slowed the stolen scooter down in order to get a grip of her emotions.

She tried to think of all the conversations she'd had with Jules about how unhappy she was—*and all the time the American whore was sleeping with my husband! Oh, how the two of them must have laughed at my expense.*

The sounds of her scooter was the only noise in the night air. She could hardly surprise the lovers if they heard her drive up! She shifted the rifle strap across her back and pulled the scooter over to the side of the road and turned off its engine.

She set the kickstand and pulled the rifle around to hold it with both hands. As she walked closer to the parked car ahead, she flashed the beam of her flashlight onto the ground until finally she saw Gaultier standing by the side of the road.

He stood with his back to the ditch watching her come.

"Who is there?" he called out.

"It is your wife, you lying bastard!" Katrine said, clutching the rifle tightly to her chest.

"Katrine?"

"Did you forget my name so soon? *Yes,* Katrine! Where is your whore?"

She was careful not to get too close but by God she wanted him to see the rifle. She wouldn't shoot him, of course. But she'd throw the fear of God into him in short order. It would be awhile before he tried this again.

"What are you doing here?" Gaultier asked. He was holding a handgun.

"What's happening?" she asked, looking in the direction of the ditch. "Where is Jules?"

"She went to relieve herself. She'll be back in a moment."

Why was he holding the gun? Was there something in the ditch?

She put the rifle to her shoulder and, aiming carefully away from Gaultier, pulled the trigger. The sound exploded in the air. The noise of it was violent and protracted and helped relieve something inside Katrine.

"You crazy bitch!" Gaultier shouted. "Have you lost your mind?"

"I don't believe your lies," she hissed. "I think your whore is in the car missing her underwear. I found them, you know, Gaultier! Her underwear! In your tool box!"

"What are you ranting about? You are demented."

"Am I?" Her voice came out plaintive and weak. She couldn't help it. Was there a possibility she was wrong? "What about the underwear? The label said they were made in the USA."

"And so you thought the American and I were sleeping together?"

When Gaultier threw back his head and laughed Katrine knew she'd gotten it wrong. The mortification was instant and pervasive.

Oh, God. What is the matter with me? Of course they weren't sleeping together. Jules was her friend. And Gaultier her loving husband.

Gaultier walked to her, the handgun now jammed into

the pocket of his workman's overalls.

"Where are the children tonight?" he asked.

"With my mother, of course. I'm sorry, Gautier. I have made a mistake."

But whose underwear were they?

For a moment she thought Gaultier wouldn't forgive her. He looked at her with such coldness in his eyes—it was almost as if she didn't know him.

"I should get back to them," she said, suddenly wanting to end this humiliating demonstration of her jealousy, her pathetic neediness.

"No. You'll come with us now."

The way he said it wasn't inviting or at all forgiving. Her scalp prickled as she tore her eyes from him to scan the ditch behind him.

Jules had been gone a long time.

"I'm only a half an hour from Chabanel," Katrine said. "It makes no sense for me to go with you to Nice."

When he came to her—as he had so many times in the past—the only thing Katrine could think was that he was finally going to forgive her for her irrational behavior. The rifle sagged in her hands as he approached. He yanked it from her hands and savagely backhanded her.

She felt her jaw explode in pain and the world rushed by her as she flew through the air, finally landing on her back on the highway. She was so stunned by what he'd done, she didn't even try to get up.

Her vision eclipsed into a pulsating light show of flashing white stars. She felt her husband on his knees beside her.

The sensation of his iron hands around her neck was almost loving as all the air in the world began to slowly ease out of her.

27

ONE TOKE OVER THE LINE

I don't know much about guns but I knew the sound of a rifle over a pistol. When I was a little girl, my uncle used to take me and my cousins to watch him skeet shoot. That's what that second gunshot sounded like to me and while I didn't immediately make the assessment that I was now hearing a different kind of firearm than before, I did figure out that if Gaultier was shooting, at least at the moment it wasn't at me.

I honestly had no idea *who* was shooting at *whom* at this point. I mean I knew Gaultier was trying to kill *me*. In fact, that's the only excuse I can give for why it took me so long to turn around and make my way back to the car to see what was going on.

And yes, I admit that a part of my impetus for returning was the dead certainty that if by some miracle I did survive this night I'd never be able to explain to *les soeurs* how I ran off and left their entire inventory of blackberry wine to be picked off by scavengers.

The closer I got to the car, the clearer it was that there were people on the road yelling at each other. I recognized

Gaultier's voice. He was speaking French which meant I didn't understand what he was saying but I could tell he was angry. He didn't sound like he was lobbying for his life. He sounded arrogant and scornful. So obviously he was still calling the shots.

That's when I recognized Katrine's voice. It was shrill and pleading.

Had Gaultier shot at his own wife? And what the hell was Katrine doing here? Had she somehow stowed away in the car? But I knew that was impossible. Between all the wine and cheese there wasn't enough room left in the car to fit a toothbrush let alone a person.

Pushing the logistics of how it was she got here, my excitement ramped up to nuclear levels at the fact that she was here.

Surely she can talk sense into her crazy murdering husband.

I slowed my steps.

Unless she's in on this with him?

This very bad thought is the only excuse I have for why it took me so long to finally peek over the rim of the ditch to see what was going on.

That's when I realized that neither of them was speaking and in fact things had been quiet for several seconds. And when I saw, illuminated in the car's headlights, the form of Gaultier leaning over Katrine's body, I thought for one crazy moment that they were making up in the time-honored way of all French people, married or not. Right up until the moment when I saw Katrine's hands feebly attempting to slap at Gaultier's hands.

The hands that were wrapped around her throat.

I was out of the ditch and running to them before I even knew I was doing it. A rifle lay beside Gaultier. I reached it just as he jerked his head around to look at me.

I swung the rifle stock straight into his surprised face.

I heard the crack of his cheekbone over the gasps of Katrine struggling for breath on the ground. Gaultier's head snapped backwards with a groan.

I flipped the rifle around and pointed it at him but I don't know anything about rifles. I didn't know if there was a safety or even if the bullets were all used up.

I saw the Luger sticking out of Gaultier's waistband but I didn't dare come close enough to try to grab it. He was recovering fast from the rifle butt to the face. I'm not that strong and it's possible the cracking sound I heard was only the sound of my mind exploding.

Blood dribbled out of his mouth and he looked at me with clarity and fury.

"You die tonight, bitch," he said, his eyes glittering with madness.

I pulled the trigger.

And heard the hammer click impotently against metal.

I pulled it again.

Nothing.

Gaultier made a roar and lunged to his feet. I didn't even have time to stagger backwards before he yanked the rifle out of my hands and threw it in the ditch. He held me by both arms, his face sinister and demented.

He was too strong for me and just acknowledging the fact seemed to weaken me further. He slapped one hand to my throat and bent my head backward. The pressure on my wind pipe was instantaneous and agonizing. White sparks danced in my now totally blackened vision.

And yet some part of my brain registered the sound of the gunshot.

The terrible pressure on my throat stopped and I felt

myself falling. The road smashed into my back, my head hitting it with a muffled thump.

I groaned and opened my eyes.

Gaultier lay face down across my legs. Over the mountainous hump of his back I saw Katrine. She was sitting up now.

And holding the Luger.

28

ONE WEEK LATER

J ust between you and me I never would have taken *les soeurs* for the sentimental types.

A week after I solved the murders of both Madame Toule and Juliette Bombre—and Katrine and I neatly disposed of the murderer himself before he could kill us—I was still being treated by the sisters as if I'd single-handedly sold every bottle of wine for twice its price.

I need to put these things into a parlance that jibes with the sisters' values, you see.

Once Katrine and I had fallen into each other's arms that terrible night and sobbed out our horror but also delight at being alive, we left Gaultier's body in the road and drove the car back to Chabanel and straight to the *police municipale.*

Luc was sleeping off a night of premature celebration but was able to rally enough to accompany Eloise to the spot on the A8 where we'd left Gaultier's body only to discover that both Gaultier and the stolen scooter had disappeared!

I know that made Katrine feel a little bit better. I'd already had a tearful earful of her *how do I tell my girls that I killed their father?* diatribe. But still—wounded or not—I wanted that S.O.B. found and punished. A.S.A.P.

It turned out I got my wish and then some. Not only did the Aix police—with that doofus Matteo riding point I'm sorry to say—find Gaultier the next night but they found him beaten to a bloody pulp where someone bigger and meaner than him had decided to take away his scooter and mess him up a little at the same time.

Karma, baby. Every time.

So while Gaultier did eventually end up getting medical care for the bullet his wife lodged into his spleen, he also got a prison cell which, after his trial, I'm pretty sure is going to translate if not into a dungeon view, then exile to the French equivalent of Van Dieman's island.

Things are changing in post-EMP France. While it's true France does still have hot croissants and can serve up an espresso with froth any time day or night, it has also decided that it no longer has the resources to house people who have proven they can't play nicely with others.

I was sitting out on the terrace at *La Fleurette*, wrapped in a thick rug that one of the Madame Twins had handmade. They sell these babies for a sizable chunk of change so while I appreciate the fact that Madame C handed it to me, I don't completely trust she won't take it back once she finds a buyer.

Cocoa stayed very close to me ever since I returned from my ill-fated road trip with Gaultier. It's almost like she knows what I've been through. She's always either curled up by my feet with her chin resting on my knee, or nearby, her eyes watching me.

Not unlike how *les soeurs* have been treating me come to think of it—minus the whole chin on the knee thing of course.

"Jules!"

I looked up from my chair to see Thibault striding through the back garden gate, a huge grin on his face. I'd seen him once after he was released and he seemed to still be riding high on his newfound freedom.

He kissed me on both cheeks and then held me in a hug for a brief moment before pulling away.

"I cannot believe any of this," he said, reaching over to tousle Cocoa's floppy ears. "You look well."

"Thanks. So do you."

"I still hate that you missed your trip home because of me."

"Well, I don't, so stop thinking about it."

Les soeurs came through the door from the house. One handed a wine bottle to Thibault with a wine opener and the other set a tray of *hors d'oeuvres* on the stone table in front of the lounge chair where I was sitting.

They spoke to Thibault and he settled himself in a chair to open the wine.

"What did they say to you?" I asked.

"What they always say to me since I am ten years old," he said with a grin. "They are happy to see me not in jail."

The sisters left the garden courtyard and returned to the house where raised voices told me that Luc had arrived. The sisters always made over Luc. I guess all the women in the village did now that I think about it.

He entered the garden from the house, carrying four wine glasses.

"*Salut*, Chief," Thibault called to him as he eased the cork out of the bottle of Côtes du Rhône.

"*Salut*, Thibault," Luc said, his eyes on me, a smile on his lips. "And *la belle* Jules."

Luc had definitely been much more flirty with me since

all this went down. I don't know what's behind it but I'm loving it. Whatever had gone on between him and Juliette—and Katrine told me she heard from Eloise that it was all a big fat nothing and that Luc felt guilty for leading Juliette on—he'd somehow come to terms with it.

Luc set the glasses on the table and leaned down to cheek kiss me. I still tingle at his touch, and the scent of lemons in some kind of very subtle after shave that's just so uniquely him.

"You look very comfortable here on your back terrace," he said. "Are you planning your spring harvest?"

"I'm not but I think the twins are. They've had workmen out here drawing lines in the dirt and digging holes and stuff. Either that or they've got a few bodies to bury."

"You still need to learn French."

"Or I could open a tutoring service to teach the whole village English," I said. "Might be simpler."

He just raised an eyebrow at me.

"I read that it's much harder to learn a language after a certain age," I said. "And, not to shock you, Luc, but I'm pretty sure I'm past that certain age."

"I could teach you."

It was the way he said it. Dead-on eye contact, a gentle arch of the eyebrow, and full-on communication in the universal language of mutual attraction.

"I'd like that," I said, trying not to pant when I said it.

The moment was interrupted by Thibault handing us both full wine glasses and raising his in a toast.

"A toast," he said. "To my very good American friend, Jules Hooker."

"Awww," I said, pleased. "It was nothing."

"It was very much not nothing," Thibault said, glancing at Luc. It occurred to me right then that Thibault would have every reason to be annoyed with Luc. After all, Luc had arrested him, detained him and packed him off to Aix.

In Luc's defense, he *had* decided to investigate Romain Armand *finally* but if that had been taken to its logical conclusion—especially in lieu of a confession which Romain most assuredly would *not* have made since he was innocent of the crime—then one innocent man would merely have been exchanged for another.

"Well, it all worked out," I said, taking a sip of wine. After drinking rosé all summer, the heavier red went straight to my head. So that was nice.

"It is really true that poor Juliette was able to get Gaultier to kill Madame Toule for her?" Thibault said, shaking his head. He already knew the facts but I couldn't blame him for not being able to wrap his head around them.

"It's true," Luc said. "She wanted vengeance on the woman she believed delivered her into the hands of a sadist."

"That would be Romain's mother, right?" I said. I knew it was right but I never tired of hearing Luc tell me over and over again of how I'd gotten it right before anyone else. It's a little thing, but hey, I wasn't getting paid for this case so yeah, I'll take it.

"*Oui*," Luc said. "Elise Toulouse was a very cold and unhappy woman. When her husband Gerard insisted they take his illegitimate child Juliette to raise, she began a campaign of abuse on the poor waif."

"And on Romain, too," I added.

"Yes, it seems, the woman was so full of hate that she failed to make the distinction between the object of her loathing and her own child."

"So when Elise Toulouse died of cancer—" I said.

"*Mais non*," Luc said. "Further investigations have revealed that Madame Toulouse died under suspicious circumstances."

"Not cancer?"

"Apparently not. Unless one of the symptoms of cancer includes blunt force trauma."

"Wow. So Juliette killed her stepmother?"

"It appears so."

"How about her father?"

Luc shrugged. "Inconclusive. A heart attack it is believed."

"But you're not sure?"

He made that annoying Gallic shrug which could mean yes or no or maybe.

"So then she went after Madame Toule, her biological mother," I said. "The one she figured was really to blame for dropping her into a life of hell."

"But why did she go to Gaultier?" Thibault said.

"Disappointed she didn't ask *you*, Thibault?" I said teasingly but felt instantly bad. Thibault had had a crush on Juliette. I'm not saying he'd kill for her. I'm nearly positive he wouldn't have, but still a guy likes to be asked, I guess.

"It appears that Pelletier and Juliette had amorously connected a few times due to their proximity at the market," Luc said. "Juliette asked him to do the deed and between the two of them they would make it look like Thibault had done it."

"Gaultier told me he killed Juliette because she wouldn't give him what she promised," I said softly.

Juliette had fallen in love with Luc and she no longer wanted to hold up her end of the bargain with Gaultier.

"Yes, that is very strange," Luc said with a frown. "They

were lovers so it is difficult to imagine why she would not reward him as promised."

"Have you asked Gaultier?" I asked.

Luc shook his head.

"He has been questioned and his confession is documented. The fact that he killed Juliette is all that matters now. Why he did it...well, why does any bad person do anything?"

"How is Katrine?" Thibault asked as he settled into one of the lounge chairs. The sun was getting ready to dip behind the fringe of firs on the far side of the pasture. It was getting darker much sooner now. The door to the house opened briefly and I could hear the babble of *les soeurs* as they put together dinner. We would eat indoors tonight.

"She's going to be okay," I said, thinking of the last time I'd seen her three days ago. We'd met briefly for coffee. Now that Gaultier was gone she truly was on her own and I think getting stronger and happier. She'd moved in with her mother for help with the two little girls and was determined to make and sell the cheese on her own.

Even after everything that had happened, when I saw Katrine—although she looked exhausted and like she'd lost about ten pounds—she appeared more at peace than I'd ever seen her. There was no doubt in my mind that even as carefully as Gaultier had kept hidden the fact that he was a murdering psycho there must have been something not too far below the surface that a wife might pick up on.

And of course Katrine being Katrine, she was only able to blame herself for her discontent because she couldn't understand what she was seeing and feeling in her marriage. She was miserable and afraid without knowing exactly why.

Now she knew.

In spades.

Katrine told me she got the scooter that night from the front of the police station where Luc had had Eloise bring it from Romain's alley. In Luc's defense, he had every reason to believe that no one in their right mind would steal a scooter parked in front of the police station.

The key phrase being, of course, *in their right mind*.

When Katrine found the offending pair of panties in Gaultier's tool box, she went mad. Her first stop was *La Fleurette* but she'd only gotten half way there before she realized not only was I not there to be dealt with but *les soeurs* would probably defend me even if I were guilty of such a crime.

Her next stop was the police station where she intended to accuse me of stealing money from her when she saw the scooter and scrapped all former plans for the much more satisfying one of riding after me and Gaultier and dispensing justice herself.

She grabbed the bike, ran home for the rifle, and then sped down the road toward Nice, fueled by pathological jealousy and rage.

When we met for coffee, I told her I couldn't believe she'd stolen a scooter from in front of a police station. I told her—as nicely and gently as I can present these things—that I thought she was probably certifiable to do such a thing.

"I was desperate," she said ruefully. "When I got it into my head that the two of you were...together...I just had to come after you. If I hadn't found the scooter I probably would've stolen old man Augustine's donkey."

"Now I would have paid money to have seen that."

"Can you ever forgive me?"

"For not trusting me? For thinking I was carrying on

with your husband? Sure. If you promise me you won't write to him in prison."

"How can you even think I would? I hate him."

I nodded. "I know. That's what I'm afraid of. You need to be a way less passionate about him."

"I'm working on it."

As Luc and Thibault and I sat outside enjoying the last glimmers of daylight, Madame Becque stepped out onto the terrace, her cardigan wrapped around her as if she were braving the atmosphere of one of the Mount Everest base camps.

"*Dîner maintenant, s'il vous plaît!*" she sang out.

Luc assured her we would be right in.

"What did you do with the blackberry wine that never made it to the Nice market?" Thibault asked.

Luc grabbed my arm. "*That's* why you were on the road with Gaultier?" he said, stunned. "You were going to the Nice special market?"

"Well, it was supposed to be a secret," I said, giving Thibault an accusing look. "But to answer your question, Thibault, *les soeurs* have agreed to sell their wine at the normal price at the Aix market." I turned to Luc. "Happy?"

He shook his head. "This just confirms to me that I have acted in your best interest. Shall we go in?"

I looked at Thibault and then back at Luc. "What are you talking about? What do you mean *my best interest*?"

Thibault spoke to Luc in French and he fired an answer back at him. I could see both of them heating up and I was confused. Damn this stupid language! Why can't everyone just speak English?

"Well, then you tell her or else I will," Thibault said to

Luc, his face red. "It is not a very nice way to be thanking her for all that she has done for you as well as for me."

"Tell me what?" I said to Luc. "What's happened? What are you two talking about?"

Luc gestured to the door of the house where both sisters were now standing. Madame Cazaly had her hands on her hips so I knew things were getting serious as far as she was concerned. You didn't let one of her meals get cold unless you were hemorrhaging and I'm sure she could see from this distance that none of us was bleeding.

"Another spot opened up on a different freighter," Thibault said calmly. "This time to New York City."

I grabbed his hand. "Another spot? I *didn't* lose my chance to go home after all? They have room for me? When? When does it leave?"

Thibault looked at me sadly. "Yesterday."

Yesterday? *Yesterday*?!

"Why didn't you tell me?" I asked him, the feeling of disappointment swelling in my chest and beginning to spread to my limbs. "Why?"

He looked from me to Luc with such a strange look on his face that I finally turned to look at Luc.

Luc was looking out at the pasture as the sun inched steadily closer to the horizon.

"I deemed it for the best," Luc said.

I stared at him for a moment, not sure I understood what he was saying.

"You deliberately didn't tell me?" I was so overcome that I had to sit back down again.

"Why?" I said in a stunned voice.

"It wasn't safe," Luc said.

"You...you don't get to decide that for me! That's *my* decision to make! *My* risk to take!"

"*Non*," he said, still not looking at me. "It isn't. I couldn't live with myself if I let you go and harm came to you."

"Couldn't...you couldn't live with..." I looked at Thibault. "There will be others? Other boats? Tell me this wasn't my last chance."

Thibault looked at me helplessly.

"I am sorry, Jules," Luc said, finally turning to look at me. "If there are other opportunities, I will block them too."

Be sure to order *A Bad Éclair Day,* the next book in the *Stranded in Provence Mysteries!*

ABOUT THE AUTHOR

USA TODAY Bestselling Author Susan Kiernan-Lewis is the author of *The Maggie Newberry Mysteries,* the post-apocalyptic thriller series *The Irish End Games, The Mia Kazmaroff Mysteries, The Stranded in Provence Mysteries,* and *An American in Paris Mysteries.*

Visit her website at www.susankiernanlewis.com or follow her at Author Susan Kiernan-Lewis on Facebook.